THE GIFT

AMANDA CAROL

This is a work of fiction. Names, characters, places, and incidents either are the product of the author's imagination or are used fictitiously. Any resemblance to actual persons, living or dead, events, or locales is entirely coincidental.

Copyright © 2020 by Amanda Carol
Cover Designer: Ashani Graphics: https://www.facebook.com/AshaniGraphics/
Editor: CPR Editing: http://www.facebook.com/cprediting
Formatter: Reader Central:

All rights reserved. No part of this book may be reproduced or used in any manner without written permission of the copyright owner except for the use of quotations in a book review.

Independently published.

To the only loves of Declan's life; Stefanie and Ciera.

"DON'T LET THE SHADOWS OF YESTERDAY SPOIL THE SUNSHINE OF TOMORROW. LIVE FOR TODAY."

NANDINA MORRIS

ONE

DECLAN

"Declan!" my sister, Aria, shouts over the loud music, snapping her fingers in front of my face.

I pull my eyes away from a sexy brunette with huge tits to look at my sister. The girl's been eye-fucking me ever since we walked in the door.

"I'm going to go for a run. I'll make sure to take my time." Aria glances at the brunette at the end of the bar, then back at me. "Please don't fuck on my bed."

It was one time that happened, and she acts like it's a huge deal. It's just sex. But then again, if I came back to the room and she was in my bed with another guy, I'd be pretty wigged out too. But in my defense, we were drunk, and I thought it was my bed.

I smirk. "I make no promises, little sis."

She rolls her eyes as I set my beer down on the countertop and pull her into a hug. There was a time when it would have pissed her off to hear me call her "little sis" or "little sister," but now it's just our thing. I think it just reminds us of a time when everything was normal.

I lean down closer to her ear. "Please be careful."

"I will," she replies, then turns and makes her way through the crowd.

I watch her take off on her run. I'm not stupid; I know why she does it. But that's neither here nor there.

I grab the beer bottle and lift it to my lips as I swivel back in my seat and glance down the bar, but that sexy brunette is gone. I slowly turn my head and scan the dance floor. My gaze connects with that pretty brunette's, but she quickly looks away at the girl she's dancing with. I spin my body around and casually lean back up against the bar, propping my elbow on the counter as I watch her dance seductively.

Give it a second.

Her eyes flick back up to mine and they darken as I finish off the rest of my beer. She sucks her bottom lip between her teeth, and without breaking eye contact with her, I set the bottle back down on the bar. I break contact first and pull out my wallet, tossing a twenty on the counter. I know that she knows I've still got my eye on her. When a woman gives me the "come and get me look," I definitely go and get her. Why wouldn't I? I get mine and she definitely gets hers.

I walk along the outskirts of the dance floor, then slowly make my way through the crowd over to her. I sidestep a drunk couple as her friend catches me approaching. The blonde leans in to whisper something in her ear and I would bet money it's to tell her that I'm right behind her.

When I grab her hips and pull her against me, she leans back, throwing her arm around my neck as she grinds her ass into my dick while her friend dances in front of her. I lean my head down, feeling her pulse quicken as my lips gently caress the side of her neck. I run the tip of my nose along her cheek; her head tilts to the side and back on my shoulder as I place my hands on her lower abdomen, right where the button on her jean skirt sits. If her mouth wasn't so close to my ear I wouldn't have heard the soft mewl sound she makes when I let her feel my growing erection.

She turns, throwing both arms around my neck, leaning in so our heads are close together. I can feel her hot breath on my cheek, and now I wish I felt it around my cock, which is starting to strain in my jeans. I turn my head ever so slightly, and when her lips gently caress mine, I push my luck and swipe my tongue on her bottom lip. She kisses me back with hunger that matches mine, and I know this chick is down for a good time.

I don't do relationships. I'm never in one place long enough to make that happen. But I would never take advantage of a woman. I let them know straight-up how it is, and if they say no, I go home alone. If they say yes, well, it's a good night for the both of us.

Have I ever fucked a girl in the bathroom? The answer is yes, but I prefer an actual room. I love hearing a woman scream my name, and I sure as hell don't want her doing that in a public restroom where we could get arrested for indecent exposure.

I don't hook up with girls all the time. Usually, when we first get into a town, I do, but after that, my sister and I hunt the vampires in town, then hit the road after we finish the job.

"Want to get out of here?" I whisper in her ear.

"Desperately," she replies breathlessly, glancing back at her friend, who is all wrapped up in another guy.

She leans in to tell her friend, who nods, then turns her attention back to her guy she's taking home tonight. I grab the brunette's hand and lead her off the dance floor and out of the bar.

When we get to my car, I stop right by the passenger door and turn to her. "Before we leave, you need to know, you can't change me. I'm just passing through town and only looking for a good time. You getting in my car tells me you understand that."

She bites her bottom lip and twirls a lock of her hair between her fingers. "Oh, I understand."

"Good," I say as one hand reaches forward and grabs her ass.

I let out a growl as I roughly pull her to me, and her breath hitches at the sudden contact. She lets out a sharp exhale through her nose as I crash my lips onto hers. She moans as I part her lips with my tongue, and her hands come up to my face. I squeeze her ass with both hands then pull away.

"Let's get the fuck out of here then..." I pause, realizing I have no idea what her name is.

"Bethany."

I smile at her, then open the door. She climbs in and I walk around to the driver seat. I've only had one beer, so I'm good to drive. And Bethany doesn't seem drunk, which is good. I don't fuck drunk girls. I might not be into relationships, but I do respect women and I wouldn't take advantage of a girl like that.

"Aren't you going to tell me your name?" she asks, turning in her seat, after I get in the car and shut the door.

"Declan." I put the key in the ignition and pull out of the parking lot.

It's late, and there aren't many other cars on the road. Bethany takes her manicured finger and runs it up my leg. The touch goes straight to my dick and I'm starting to feel confined in my jeans, more so than on the dance floor.

I glance over at her and she tugs her bottom lip between her teeth again. I let my eyes briefly trail down her body, noticing her chest is flushed, and I don't think it's from the dancing. I clench my jaw as she unbuckles her seatbelt and reaches over to undo the button of my pants.

"You want to live dangerously for one night?" she says, looking up at me through thick lashes and rubbing my dick through my pants.

"Sweetheart, I live dangerously every night," I reply truthfully.

Getting road head is dangerous if you've never done it before, but it's definitely not my first time.

She giggles. "I just bet you do."

She unzips me, wrapping her hand around my cock and pulling it out of my boxers. I inhale sharply and my cock starts to throb in her hand as she gives it a light squeeze.

Fuck, please, just put...atta girl.

When her tongue licks the tip of my dick, I swerve a little bit, but catch myself and focus on the road.

She wraps her mouth around me and begins to bob her head up and down. With one hand on the steering wheel, the other moves the hair out of her face because she's working me with both her hands and her mouth. I grip the steering wheel, and I push down on her head a little bit. When my cock hits the back of her throat, I can feel her gag, so I pull back, and place both hands on the wheel. I can see the entrance to the motel, and I'm so fucking ready to put this goddamn car in park so I can really enjoy this.

Finally, I pull into a dark parking spot, throw the car in park, and lean back, thrusting my hips forward. She moans on my cock, and the vibration combined with her working my dick causes my balls to tighten.

"Fuck," I breathe. "I'm going to come."

I always like to warn the women who suck my dick when I'm about to come. Not every girl likes to swallow, and it seems like this girl is one of those girls who doesn't like to because she removes her mouth, making that sexy "pop" noise, but continues to jerk me off. I pull the bottom of my shirt over my dick to clean up the mess, then I carefully take off my shirt off and ball it up before tucking myself back into my jeans.

I look over at her. "We aren't finished."

I get out of my car, and she follows me to my room. I toss my shirt over on my suitcase next to my hoodie when we get inside. I turn to find Bertha standing by the door. *Is that her name?*

"Who else is with you?" she asks, looking at my sister's bed with her things on it.

Her tone is a little accusatory, but at this point, I'm really just trying to get laid.

"My sister. She's going to be out for a while." I walk over to her and grab her hand.

I bring her further into the room and, not wanting to lose the momentum, I kiss her. Her fingers trace down my abs, and then they make their way up to my chest, then over my shoulders. I let my hands fall to her hips, and grabbing the hem of her shirt, I lift it over her head.

Damn.

Her tits are glorious.

I place my hand over her tit, and my fingers tweak her nipple through her red lacy bra. If a girl has on a matching bra and panties, she definitely decided she was having sex tonight before you came along.

She moans into my mouth and presses her chest against mine. I reach around her back, and with the snap of my fingers, her bra comes undone. The straps slide down her shoulders and I kiss her neck as I pull it off her. I walk us backward toward my bed and I sit as soon as my legs hit the mattress. She kicks off her shoes and straddles me, grinding her hips into my erection. I've got a tit in one hand and my other goes up into her skirt.

Fuck me. She's not wearing any panties.

I start to swirl my thumb around her clit when the door bursts open.

"Oh, my God!" Aria yells, covering her eyes.

Betsy squeals, jumping up quickly from my lap and grabbing the closest blanket.

"Jesus! Aria! Ever heard of knocking?" I shout, bending over and grabbing a shirt from off the floor, careful not to grab the one that I had used to clean myself off with.

It's the one I had on earlier before I changed to go to the bar. My lady friend starts looking for her clothes and I toss her shirt at her after she puts her bra back on. I look over at my sister, who still has her eyes covered, but her fingers part, and she removes her hand from her face when she notices we are both fully dressed.

"Um, Declan, who is this?" Becca asks, looking really annoyed. One could possibly even say a little jealous.

I'm not sure why she's jealous. I *told* her that the other bed was my sister's, and Aria is my identical twin, for fuck's sake. A fact which stumped the doctors and even me. Aria and I are a unique breed of human, since it's extremely rare for a set of identical twins like us to be born.

"Is she serious right now?" Aria asks, her brows raised.

I can see the humor in her pale green eyes and my lips turn up slightly. I run a hand through my platinum blonde hair, then glance down at my sister's shirt.

What the fuck?

She's covered in blood.

Aria tries to cross her arms over her body to hide it, but I don't think she really needs to since Beatrice hasn't even noticed it. I guess it shouldn't surprise me that much since she still hasn't grasped that Aria and I are siblings. I just wanted to get laid. But now I'm sort of happy with the interruption. I walk across the room and grab my hoodie and toss it at my sister. Then I turn to the girl standing awkwardly in the room.

"Look, Brittany—"

"It's Bethany," she corrects me, rolling her eyes.

"Right, Bethany," I say, walking across the room, picking up her shoes, and handing them to her. "I think you'd better go."

"You cannot be serious!" she hisses through clenched teeth as she snatches her shoes out of my hands and puts them on. "Why doesn't *she* come back later?"

I whip my head in my sister's direction and I can already see the wheels turning in her head. I shoot her a pleading look to not say anything. I just want this girl to leave already. But if I know Aria, and I do, she's not going to let it go.

Aria narrows her eyes. "*She* has a name. And if I'm not mistaken, Declan asked you to leave. Not me. So, take the hint, Becky."

My sister totally just fucked up her name on purpose, and it takes everything in me not to laugh.

After a long stare down with my sister, Bethany comes over, grabs my face, and crashes her lips onto mine. She forces her tongue into my mouth, and I try not to kiss her back. Thankfully, she pulls away rather quickly and motions for me to call her.

Yeah, not going to happen. Actually, I didn't even get her number.

As soon as the door shuts behind her, Aria bursts out laughing.

"Oh, my God. Declan, that was great. She's a keeper. You should totally put a ring on it." She walks further into the room.

"Yeah, well, girls like her are easy. All you have to do is tell them they're beautiful and that they can do anything they set their mind to. Hook, line, and sinker." I wink. I didn't have to do that tonight, but the tactic does work.

"That's horrible. I can't wait for the day when one girl walks into your life and changes everything," Aria says.

"I doubt that'll ever happen. We're never in one place long enough for me to even consider something serious. I just happen to like sex. And I never lead girls on. I let them know up front what the deal is. I'm not a total tool. Maybe you should try taking a page out of my book. You might not be so uptight," I joke.

I know why Aria lets me have nights to myself. She won't ever tell me, but I know. She does it because I'm the one who got us out of our parents' room that night a vampire killed our parents.

"Anyway," I finally say after I notice Aria look nervously at the floor. "Do you mind telling me what in the actual fuck happened out there tonight?"

I walk over and stand right in front of her. I tilt her face up, and notice she's getting a nice bruise on her cheek.

"A vampire attacked a girl tonight," she whispers.

I take a step back from her. A mixture of emotions hit me all at once as I process what that means. She fucking fought a vamp *by herself*. And clearly it didn't work out so well, since she's covered in blood. I could have lost her.

"Fuck! What happened to the plan, Aria? You were supposed to follow the SOB and then come and get me. We never go after a vampire alone. It's too dangerous!" I shout, running my hands through my hair. "How could you do this? What if he killed you? Huh?"

I can't do this without her. She's all the family I have left. She never stops to think about what she does before she does it.

"I know! I didn't think—" she starts to say.

"You're damn right you didn't think!" I cut her off.

"He was killing this poor girl. I just acted on instinct! Was I supposed to let her die?" Aria yells back at me.

We have a typical Matthews glare-off. The look on her face lets me know that she doesn't need me to make her feel any more guilty than she already does.

"No, but you were supposed to be smart about it," I sigh, coming back over and pulling her to me. She wraps her arms around my waist, and I rest my chin on her head. "God, Aria, the moment I saw you covered in blood earlier..."

I know I don't have to finish that statement.

"He's dead," Aria states flatly, and pulls away to go over to her backpack. She pulls out some ibuprofen and pops two in her mouth, swallowing them.

"You killed him? By yourself?" I ask, kind of surprised.

But I know my sister; she can fight. We've just never killed a vamp without the other person there before.

"Yes. I can handle myself in a fight, Declan. Why is that so surprising?" she defends and walks over to her suitcase, pulling out fresh clothes.

"Aria, stop. I didn't mean it like that," I say, blocking her path to the bathroom.

She stops and narrows her eyes at me. I'm not angry with her. I'm proud that she was able to save a life, but what if she wasn't able to?

"I'm sorry, okay? I know you can take care of yourself. I've seen you fight and you're a badass fighter. I just..." I pause, letting out a harsh breath. "Please, just don't do that to me again. I saw the blood on you and I...I can't lose you too."

"You won't lose me. I promise I won't do that again. I love you too, bro. Even if you are a man-whore." She pats my shoulder.

I laugh.

"Now that we've had this whole heart-to-heart moment, can you please move? I'd like to not look like I just walked out of a horror film," she jokes, lightening the mood.

I move out of her way. I know the cuts and bruises she has will be almost healed by the morning. It's weird, but after our parents died, we became faster and stronger. I mean, I was already strong because of sports, but now I'm stronger than normal. We also heal more quickly than average humans. Of course, I questioned it at first, but then I figured it didn't matter why. As long it helps us fight vampires, who cares where these new abilities came from?

I walk over to the little table in the room and open my laptop. Earlier, I was looking up the usual animal attack news articles, but ended up getting off-track and found that New Orleans hasn't seen any suspicious deaths lately. Like, not a single one.

The door to the bathroom opens and Aria walks out and over to me. As soon as she gets behind me, she slaps a hand over her eyes.

"Oh, God! You aren't watching porn, are you? I think I've seen enough for one lifetime!" She laughs as she pulls her hand away from her face.

"Ha-ha. You're so funny," I reply sarcastically.

"I'm hilarious. So, got anything new?" she asks.

"I'm not sure. I haven't had anything new come across as far as vampire attacks are concerned. But check this out. I was looking for the usual and the unusual came up," I tell her.

She gives me a confused look, and I sigh.

"I've been researching the norm. You know, trying to find articles about animal attacks. But I found this article about New Orleans. They haven't had an animal attack in over a decade. Which sounds weird to me. I'm not sure, but I really feel like maybe we should check this out." I rub my fingers against my chin as I stare at the computer screen.

"Okay, we should check it out. Your instincts have always been on point. It wouldn't hurt to stop by," Aria comments as she walks over to her night table and grabs her hairbrush.

"It'll take us at least eight hours to get there, though," I reply, getting lost in thought. If we leave here around seven, we should get there around nightfall, and we'll have time so scope the place out.

"We can leave first thing in the morning. We can take turns driving too, so we can get there quicker," Aria suggests, yawning and crawling into her bed.

"Yeah, okay, sounds good." I shut my laptop and walk over to my bed, trying to form a plan for the drive and stay.

Aria is sound asleep as soon as her head hits the pillow, but as I lie awake, I start to get the feeling that our lives are about to change forever.

Two

CIERA

Be a teacher, they said. It'll be fun, they said.

Ha! It's a great day to be me right now. Lucas pulled Callie's hair and she used her power of air to push him. Then Tucker thought it would be funny to stick a Lego up his nose, where it proceeded to get stuck.

"Hold still, Tucker." I tell him.

He starts to get fussy as I hold his head back. I tilt his head back even further, and with tweezers, I carefully pull the Lego out.

"There, all better. Now go and play."

"Fanks, Ms. Campbell!" Tucker squeals, wiping his nose.

The poor little guy still struggles with his pronunciation of T's. We're working on it.

"And don't stick any more Legos up your nose!" I shout at him as he runs away.

"Boys are gross." Maggie, the princess, comes over and sits down. "They have cooties!"

I smile at her. "Aww, Mags, that's not very nice. Boys don't have cooties."

"Yes-huuuuh," she drawls, rolling her big brown eyes. "Tucker stuck a Lego up his nose! And I saw Thomas eat a booger!"

I scrunch my nose. That *is* really gross.

"Well, that's still not a very nice thing to say." I look down at her and quirk a brow. "Did you clean up your nap area yet?"

"Yes," she says, but I can tell from the look on her face that she just lied to me.

"Maggie." I cross my arms over my chest.

"O-tay. I'm going now." Maggie sags her shoulders and sulks over to her mat.

It's moments like this I wouldn't ever trade. I love my kids, and I love teaching them. Every single one of them has a unique personality, some stronger than others. Maggie is my fearless ringleader, but she is also gentle and kind like her best friend Callie. Tucker is one of my youngest, along with Callie's little sister, Peyton. The littlest ones are my biggest troublemakers.

I love being a teacher. It's the best feeling knowing that I'm making a difference in their lives.

I only teach the young ones, ages three to eight. Then they move on to someone else. When a witch is born, they don't come into their powers until about the age of three. Sometimes earlier, sometimes later, but that's what I'm here for. I teach them to control their powers, how to calm themselves and not let their emotions influence their magic. But I also teach academic skills as well, since putting them in a public school is a disaster waiting to happen. Not that it doesn't happen, but witches tend to homeschool their children until they gain control of their powers.

I have different lesson plans for each age. For half the day, we focus on the magic, then nap time because using magic can take a toll on their little bodies. After that, we start working on the academic stuff.

Witches can work out in the real world with humans, and I love giving these kids the opportunity to go to college so they can live a normal life if they want to. My parents gave that to me, but they don't like being witches.

They have to live very carefully out in the world, because our blood is like a drug to vampires. Well, that's how my grandma put it, before we moved here from Texas.

"Ms. Campbell! Ms. Campbell!" Maggie calls.

I quickly look over and see her pointing at Tucker who has a mischievous grin on his face and another Lego in his hand. The other boys are surrounding him, giggling and egging him on.

"Tucker!" I shout.

He jumps, dropping the Lego on the ground.

"Legos are not meant to be stuck anywhere but to each other," I scold.

He and the other boys scatter and start to play with the toy cars.

"I swallowed a Lego once," Joey says nonchalantly, taking a sip of juice out of his juice box.

I look down at him, expecting him to elaborate.

He doesn't.

"Alright everybody, grab your backpacks, it's time to take you guys home!" I yell out.

They all run over to their little cubbies and grab their things. I don't have a huge class. There are only about seven kids here under the age of ten. They line up, and I make them all hold hands as we exit the schoolhouse. I pick them up in the morning and take them home in the afternoon. We live rent-free, and we even have a cafeteria to help feed us. The wolf shifters use the cafeteria the most, because of their patrolling shifts. The city of New Orleans hasn't had a vampire attack in a long time and that's all because of the wolf pack.

I drop Joey off first.

His mother, Katey, waves at me. "Thank you!"

I wave back at her just before she closes the door. Callie and Peyton get dropped off next, and one by one I drop the kids off. I finally get to Maggie's house and I knock on the door a few times, but it seems as though no one is home. Her parents own a shop in the Quarter, like some of the people here do. I see her little shoulders fall and she frowns. Her parents adore her, and they try to get home in time for her, but sometimes they don't. The storm really took a toll on everyone here, especially those that have stores or work jobs in the city.

"Want to go for a snack?" I ask her, and her face lights up.

"Can I have ice cream?" she asks, sticking out her bottom lip.

"I'm not sure your parents will like that. How about we share some veggies and dip?" I offer.

She makes a face. I try to get my students to eat healthy snacks during the day. But I'm a hypocrite, because during their nap time I sneak and eat some chips and chocolate.

"French fries?"

"Can we dip them in chocolate ice cream?" Maggie asks excitedly as I open the door to the barn.

I laugh. That does actually sound amazing. "Okay, fine."

"Yes!" she shouts, and all eyes look at us.

The training room door opens, and the shifters and witches all walk out. The Alpha, Alexander, requires all witches and shifters to train starting at the ripe age of thirteen. I moved here when I was younger and had to go through the course. The witches have the option to opt out when they finish the required courses.

Hunter, the Alpha's son, spots me and walks over.

"Hey, Ciera." He glances down at Maggie, then kneels so he's eye level with her. "Why hello, Miss Maggie May. How are you today?"

She looks up at him. "I'm great! Ms. Campbell is getting us some French fries and some chocolate ice cream to dip them in!"

He lifts a brow at me.

"What? It's my weakness," I say.

Hunter chuckles as his best friend, Bennett, walks over.

"'Sup, guys?" He glances down at Maggie, who had just grabbed a plate, and squints his eyes at her. "Maggie."

She looks up and squints her eyes back. "Bennett."

"I told you, the next time I see you, it's on." Bennett watches as Maggie carefully sets her plate down and goes over to him.

She holds her palm out with one hand and puts her tiny little fist above it. Bennett stands a little taller and mimics her position. Hunter and I share amused looks and take a step back.

"On three." Bennett says.

Maggie nods.

"One," he starts.

"Two." Maggie narrows her eyes.

"Three," they say together.

They smack their fists in their hands three times. On the fourth, Bennett holds his fist out, and Maggie's hand goes flat.

"Paper beats rock! I win!" Maggie squeals and giggles.

Bennett's eyes grow wide and he takes a step back. "Evil. She's evil."

"Benny, maybe if you picked something other than rock, you might actually win." Hunter pinches the bridge of his nose.

Bennett scoffs. "I don't always use rock. I switch it up with some scissors." Then he looks at Maggie. He takes two fingers and points them at his eyes, then at her.

Maggie giggles and picks her plate back up.

"I'm going to go try and get a quick nap in before we go out tonight. Laters," he announces.

I glance over at Hunter. "Patrolling tonight?"

"Yeah. He's got the right idea, though. You ladies enjoy your French fries and chocolate ice cream." Hunter gives me a hug, then turns to leave.

When I first arrived here, Hunter and Bennett took me under their wings. I was always following them asking them questions about being a wolf. Bennett always called me the "curious little witch." He doesn't anymore, thank goodness.

I help Maggie put fries on the plate and I get us a scoop of chocolate ice cream, and we make our way over to one of the tables to enjoy our afternoon treat.

"This is the best day ever." Maggie shuts her eyes as she savors everything. "Thank you, Ms. Campbell."

"Maggie?" I say, wondering something.

"Hmm?"

"Did you know that Bennett was going to choose rock?" I ask.

Her eyes flick up to mine and she smiles really big. "Yes. He always chooses rock. But he likes to switch to scissors on time number three. Every time. He never chooses paper." She dips another fry in the ice cream.

I balk at her. "Child, you are too smart for your own good. Where is this effort in class?"

Maggie shrugs. "Because playing rock, paper, scissors is fun. School is not. I do like magic, though. That is fun."

She's too engrossed in her food to look up at me. I'm slightly offended because I've always loved school. I guess I always thought the other kids felt the same way. Turns out, I was wrong.

We finish up, and I walk Maggie back to her cabin. Her parents are home and I tell them what we just ate. They don't mind, and they thank me profusely for watching after her a little while longer. I smile, wave goodbye to them, and walk back to my cabin.

"Hello, my darling girl. How was your day?" my grandma, Kora, asks as I shut the door and walk in the kitchen.

I sniff the air, and she's making chicken and dumplings. She's got on her long pink robe and matching slippers. Her long gray-blonde hair is pulled neatly back into a bun.

"Interesting, to say the least." I kiss her cheek and go to lift the ladle to have a taste of one of my favorite meals, but she slaps my hand away.

"I didn't raise a heathen. Now, get out of my way while I finish this up," she scolds, but I know she doesn't mean it.

"How was your day, Grandma?" I ask, sitting down at the table.

"Oh, it was a lovely day. I went into town for some more supplies with Luna and her wonderful daughter Abby. I did have to tend to a witch who got a little too into it in that training class."

I cross my legs under me in the chair as I listen to her tell me all about her day. After a few minutes she turns.

"Oh, I'm sorry, my dear. Listen to me ramble on, please tell me how the children were today."

I smile. "They were great. Although Tucker did stick a Lego up his nose. Callie used the air element to push Lucas back for pulling her hair. As impressive as it was, I still had to put her in time-out. The kids are getting better at controlling their power, but sometimes their emotions overwhelm them."

"Yes, that will happen. I believe a certain young witch would sneak into the kitchen and use her power to bring the cookie jar to her when she was told no. Could never keep you away from the sweets. Your mama fussed at me for keeping the jar on the counter, but it didn't matter where I put it. You'd always find it." My grandma narrows her eyes at me, then gives me a warm smile, leaning in close. "Me and your daddy would always hide it in easy places." Then she winks.

I return her smile and lean back into my chair. I do love sweets. I remember when we were really little, Hunter would always get three cookies. One for me, one for him, and we would split the third. He is the best honorary big brother. The same can be said for Bennett. He would always cover me up on the couch and let me snuggle close as we watched a movie together. His commentary would always make me giggle.

When dinner is ready, we eat together and then I clean up while she goes to watch *Young and the Restless,* her favorite soap opera. Sometimes I'll watch it with her, but I usually go up to my room and work on lesson plans for the next day. After I put the leftovers in the fridge, I grab my messenger bag and go up to my room. I sit down at my desk, pulling out my lesson planner, and pop my headphones in. I go to the marked page and begin to work on tomorrow's lesson plan.

I check my watch when I hear a loud knock on the front door. It's late, and that usually means something happened on a patrol. I close my lesson planner and go downstairs.

"Hey, Kora. Hunter asked me to get you. We ran into these humans tonight and one of them got beat up pretty bad. Can you come to the barn?" Bennett asks, running a hand through his hair.

Grandma turns to me. "I'll be back soon."

She leaves with Bennett. I glance down and realize that she forgot her medical bag. I run up to my room, grab a hoodie because it can get cold in the medical room, and put my Converse on. I don't usually wear them. Typically I stick to flip-flops or flats. I grab Grandma's bag, open the door, and jump back as soon as I run into a hard body.

"For goodness' sake, Bennett! You scared the crap out of me!" My heart is still racing in my chest.

"Sorry. Kora wanted me to grab you too. In my defense, I was about to knock," Bennett says as I step out onto the porch, shutting the door behind me.

I shoot him a dirty look, and he laughs.

"Yeah, she forgot her medical bag, so I was going to bring it to her," I reply as we make our way over to the barn. "What happened?"

"We met these twins at St. Louis Cemetery, Aria and Declan. Declan got knocked out by a vampire and hit his head pretty bad. Blondie is a badass and helped us kill the bloodsucker. They know about us too, and witches," Bennett explains.

"Blondie?" I ask. Bennett and his nicknames.

"Oh, that would be Aria," Bennett replies just as we reach the barn door.

He opens it for me, and we make our way over to the medical room. There is a platinum blonde girl standing next to a cot with an identical-looking man laying down. This must be Aria and Declan. He's got a nasty looking head wound and he looks like he went a few rounds with Blaine, the Compound's resident shifter jerk.

"Here, Grandma," I say, handing my grandma her medical kit.

She takes it from me and starts to rummage through it.

"What do you need me to do?" I look at the twins briefly before turning my attention back to my grandmother.

"Here, Ciera. Take this," Grandma commands.

I take the gauze and the paste concoction we use to help slow the bleeding. Grandma makes most of them and we only know one by name, everything else is by color. This one is yellow, and kind of reminds of me mustard.

"Put this on his wound. It'll help stop the bleeding. I'm going to make Gumba Paste to help speed up the healing process then mix a potion to help with the concussion," she finishes.

I nod and walk over to the man lying on the cot, and I place the gauze on his head. When he turns to look at me, his gaze softens. I look down at him, studying his sharp jawline and high cheekbones. When our eyes meet, I take note of the pale green color. I'm surrounded by gorgeous guys, shifters and witches alike, but this guy...he's different.

"You're an angel," he says, smiling. "I must be in heaven."

He grins, placing his hand on top of mine, and closes his eyes. I glance at his sister; her long platinum blonde hair is pulled back into a ponytail and she's giving her brother a weird look. I look behind her at Hunter, who is only watching her. I've never seen Hunter look at a girl like this before. It looks like he wants to wrap her up in a blanket and keep her safe, or he wants to kiss her. Either way, I think Hunter might be crushing on this girl. Declan pats my hand, pulling my attention back to him, and opens his eyes again.

"You're beautiful," Declan whispers.

"Thanks, Romeo." I smile. "But I think you've bumped your head a little too hard. Let's get you patched up, okay?"

This isn't the first time I've had to deal with situations like this. Kai hits on me all the time, and while it was charming at first, it got rather annoying. Kai is hot and a great guy, but I've known him for years. I just don't see him in that way.

"You have the voice of an angel too!" Declan says, then turns to look at his sister. "Psst! Aria! I think I met the woman of my dreams."

He closes his eyes, then opens them to look at me once more. His green eyes sparkle in the overhead lights.

"What's your name?" he asks. Even loopy, he still packs on the charm.

"Ciera."

"Such a beautiful name for a beautiful woman," Declan sighs.

I chuckle, but it goes unnoticed because Grandma comes back over with Gumba Paste and a cup full of the potion that will heal his concussion. It's absolutely revolting. I would know because I've needed to drink it before. I quickly move out of her way as she cleans his head up and places the Gumba Paste on his wound. I can feel Declan's eyes on me when I grab the bloody gauze and throw it away.

"Drink this. It's not going to taste good, but it'll help ease the pain and heal that concussion you have," I hear Grandma explain.

When she hands Declan the small cup, Abby and Aria help him sit up as he takes the cup from her. He drinks it quickly but makes a face and looks like he might spit it back out.

"I don't know what ass tastes like, but if I had to guess, I imagine that's exactly what it would taste like," Declan groans.

I have to hold in the laugh that's starting to bubble up in my chest. I've heard a lot of things about the way that potion tastes, but it being compared to *that* is new.

I hear Bennett start laughing behind me, and Grandma narrows her eyes at him. She uses the air element to "smack" him on the head, a trick I've been trying to learn, but can't ever master. I can slam and lock doors, but smacking someone with air takes a lot of focus and practice. It took Grandma years to perfect it.

"Ouch!" Bennett hisses, rubbing his head. "What'd you do that for? Hunter was laughing too!"

Grandma threatens him again, but he holds his hands up.

As Grandma shoos everyone out of the room, I sneak off and go over to the cafeteria. Aria looks tired and hungry and could probably use a warm meal. I figure you can't go wrong with a burger and fries. That's the southern hospitality for you.

I take it out to her, then walk back inside the medical room and see Grandma sitting behind her desk organizing her medical kit.

"I'm heading back. Need anything before I go?" I ask her.

"Mm-hmm, that's quite alright dear," she answers, counting her gauze packs, then recounting them.

"I'll be back in a few hours to relieve you. Love you." I lean in and kiss her cheek.

She lets me, then continues her counting. Curiosity gets the best of me when I glance over at Declan. My legs are moving before my brain makes the decision to walk over there.

His face is cast in shadows, but I can still make out his features. He finally fell back asleep, so I lift the gauze off his head to check to see if the paste is working. My curiosity is piqued when I look at his almost completely healed head wound. Our potions and pastes are good, but not that good. The only other time I've seen wounds heal this quickly is on a wolf shifter. He's not a shifter, but I'm beginning to suspect that he's not human either.

Three

CIERA

Witches can sense power in each other. I've been around magic my whole life, so I know when I'm around a person with power. Declan has power, but it feels… muted, somehow.

He moans and shifts, and the light reflects off his necklace. I can't believe I didn't even notice that before. Then my eyes trail down, and that's when I realize he's not wearing a shirt. I'm used to being around shirtless men, living on the Compound, so I guess with the chaos of the evening, I never really noticed it. He's not extremely muscular like the shifters, but the guy is still muscular, and toned… and gorgeous.

Focus, Ciera.

I reach forward and pick up the sun-shaped pendant hanging from a chain around his neck. It wields powerful magic. The spell that was used to make this probably came with a pretty high price, since all enchantments or spells that go against the balance of nature come with a consequence. My eyes snap up to his face when he moves his head once more and I gently lay the pendant back down on his chest. This is binding magic, but why is he wearing something that would bind his powers? He's not a witch or a shifter.

"What are you?" My voice is barely above a whisper.

"What was that, dear?"

I jump at the sound of Grandma's voice and spin around.

"Nothing. I'll see you later," I say as I rush out of the medical room and back to our cabin.

I slam the door shut behind me and rush back upstairs to my room and kick off my shoes. I toss my hair into a messy bun and start to pace.

I know what he's not.

I know that he's not a human.

"What am I missing?" I say out loud, as I continue to pace.

Just then, I hear a knock on my front door. Ugh. Now what? I rush back downstairs and am surprised to see Kai standing there.

"Hey, Ci-Ci." Kai smiles at me.

"I told you not to call me that." I roll my eyes, pulling my hair out from my messy bun. "What are you doing here?"

"Bennett told me to drop these off with you," he replies, holding up a set of car keys.

"Oh." I reach forward and take the keys from him. "Thank you. What car is it for?"

"You're welcome, beautiful. And it's the Honda HRV. I parked it next to your Jeep." Kai smirks, crossing his arms over his broad chest. A dark curl falls flat on his forehead, and he swivels his head to get it off.

"Thanks again, Kai." I smile at him.

His smirk disappears as a breeze whips my hair in front of my face. He reaches forward and tucks a lock behind my ear, then his hand cups my cheek. I make the mistake of letting my gaze meet his and he starts to lean forward. His eyes start to glow as he gets closer. A shifter's eyes only glow if they feel an intense emotion.

Oh, no.

Abort! Abort! Abort!

"Kai," I whisper.

He rests his forehead against mine. "I know. I just wish you'd give me a chance."

I pull out of his grasp. "It's not that, Kai. I just don't see you in that way, and I don't want to ruin our friendship."

I cringe at my word choice because I totally just put him in the friend zone. He's such a sweetheart and will make one lucky lady happy someday. I've had relationships before, but I want passion. I want someone who will challenge me and ask the deep questions. I want the next guy to get to know my mind first, then my body. Kai isn't that person, and I feel bad, but I can't help how I feel about him.

"I understand." Kai leans forward and kisses my cheek. "Goodnight, Ciera."

"Goodnight, Kai," I reply.

I watch as he shifts into his wolf and runs off into the night. I shut the door and walk back up to my room, twirling the car keys in my hand.

I need to think outside the box.

I know the history of witches comes from the Greek gods. They would gift mortals with an elemental power if they were worthy. I know that wolf shifters were created by Artemis to balance out what Apollo did with the first vampire.

What am I missing?

Grabbing a Greek mythology textbook from my bookshelf, I sit back down at my desk and start reading. When I check the time, it's about three in the morning. I place a bookmark in the page I was reading and slip my shoes back on. I grab the car keys and make my way over to the parking lot to the twins' Honda HRV. I assume the purple backpack is Aria's and the black Under Armor one is Declan's. I open it and see there's a change of clothes, so I don't have to rummage through their things to find him some fresh clothes. I pull out my phone and text Jasper that I left the car door unlocked, asking if he would take the rest of their things to Luna's cabin.

"Hey, Grandma, I'm here now. Why don't you go back to the cabin to rest for a while? I'll keep an eye on Declan," I say as I enter the medical room.

I set Declan's backpack down on the floor and set the book down on the desk, startling Grandma.

"What did I say about doing that! You gave me a fright, almost made the old ticker stop beating." Grandma clutches her chest, but I can see the corners of her lips tip up in a smile.

"That old ticker won't give out anytime soon," I giggle as she gets up and grabs her robe from the hook.

"You're right. You going to be all right here by yourself?" she asks as she pulls the robe closed.

"Yes, I'll be fine." I shoo her off and sit in the chair, opening the textbook back up.

"Alright, I'll see you later then. Bye, sweetheart." Grandma kisses the top of my head, grabs her bag, and leaves me alone in the room.

I start reading the book again, skimming through the history I already know. I get to the chapter about demigods, but I hear a groan from across the room. I glance up and see that Declan is starting to wake up, so I place the bookmark between the pages and set the book down. I get up, quickly grabbing some ibuprofen and a glass of water and walk over to him.

"Where am I?" he asks in a low, husky voice. "Fuck, my head hurts." He reaches up and touches the bandage on his head, and his eyes grow wide. "Wait. Where is my sister?"

He suddenly sits up and is out of the bed quickly, knocking the glass out of my hand. I jump out of the way, but I notice Declan tumble to the ground a few feet away.

"Whoa! Hey!" I shout, rushing over to him, trying to not step on the glass.

"I have to find my sister. Where is she?" Declan gets back up and starts to rush for the door.

I can't let him, not while he's still healing. Without thinking, I use the air element to slam the door shut. Declan halts in his tracks and I use the air element again to bolt the door.

"You are in no condition to walk right now; your body went through some trauma and it's trying to heal," I say.

He slowly turns to me, and the look on his face isn't fear. He's looking at me so intensely that I start to flush under his gaze. A guy has never looked at me quite like this before.

"You're a witch, aren't you?" he asks, and I remember Bennett telling me that they know about shifters, witches and vampires.

I nod. "Yes."

"And my sister? Where is she?"

"She's safe with someone who lives here, Abby Thibodaux. They seem to know each other," I tell him, and he seems to calm.

"Brown hair, gray eyes, and about yay tall?" He positions his hand at chest level.

"That's the one," I reply, not sure where this conversation is going to go.

"How do I know you're not lying?" Declan asks, taking a step back.

"You're just going to have to trust me. Hunter and Bennett brought you guys back here, and we had your car and belongings delivered here as well. Abby texted me a few hours ago and said that Aria was fast asleep. I promise you, she's safe."

"Are Hunter and Bennett witches?" he asks, slowly walking back toward me.

"No," I say just as he reaches me.

His eyes search my face for a moment before glancing behind me.

"I'm sorry about the broken glass. My sister is the only family I have left, and I—" His voice breaks as he looks down at me.

"It's okay. I understand," I whisper, giving him a small smile. "Would you mind if I changed your bandages?"

He smirks. "You're the nurse. You do what you need to do."

"Go lie back down. I'll be right over," I command.

He goes back over to his cot, careful not to step on the broken glass. I grab some more ibuprofen, water in a plastic cup this time, extra gauze, and some more Gumba Paste.

"Here, take this." I hand him the pills and water.

"Thanks." He throws the pills in his mouth and takes a large gulp of water.

"You're welcome." I smile as he hands me the cup. I take it back to the desk, then walk back over. "I'm going to check your head wound now and clean it up a bit. Is that okay?"

He nods, then winces as I start to take the bandage off.

"I'm sorry," I say. "I know this must hurt."

"Actually, it's not so bad. You don't have to be careful with me. You can rip it off if you want to. I've been through worse." Declan's eyes meet mine, and I can tell he's being serious even though his tone sounds sarcastic. "I'm Declan, by the way. What's your name?"

I stop what I'm doing. "You don't remember?"

His eyes grow wide. "Please don't tell me I had diarrhea of the mouth." His head falls back down on the pillow and he closes his eyes. "You told me your name and I don't even remember it. If my sister was here, she'd be giving me so much shit right now."

I chuckle and glance at his wound, noticing that it's just about healed up.

Yeah, he's definitely not just a human.

I suck in a breath. "I'm going to leave the bandage off and let this get some air. In the meantime, I'll go and grab us something to eat. Are you hungry?"

"Sounds good, and yeah I could eat." He smiles at me as I turn to walk over to the desk to throw the used gauze in the trash.

"I hope you don't mind, but I grabbed your backpack out of your car. I'm sure you'll want something to change into." I bring over the backpack and hand it to him, then grab the broom, dustpan and some paper towels to clean up the mess.

"Thank you. I appreciate it," he says as he watches me clean the broken glass and spilled water. "I can help you with that."

"No, that's okay. I've got it. You need to rest," I reply, using my foot to wipe the floor. Once I'm finished, I throw the glass and the used paper towels away and turn to face him. "Okay, I'm going to grab us some breakfast now. Want anything in particular?"

"Your name."

I smile. "Ciera."

He returns my smile before I spin around and head for the door.
"Hey, Ciera," he calls out.
I turn again, lifting a brow.
"Surprise me," he says.

Four

Declan

I watch the door close behind Ciera and lean my head back onto the pillow. I have no fucking clue why I trust her.

I knew something was off with Hunter and Bennett when we met them in the cemetery. The last thing I remember was them following Aria and I back in after we heard the scream. That was when I realized that they had to know about vampires.

I have no idea what happened after I got knocked out, but I trust the girl—or should I say, witch—with the long blonde hair and the most beautiful blue eyes I've ever seen. I know my track record with remembering women's names, but her name isn't a name that I would *want* to forget, and I'm not sure why. There's just something about her that's different. Maybe it's because she's a witch, or the fact that my charm didn't make her bat an eye. I mean, she's gorgeous and just my type, but there's something else there.

Opening up my bag, I grab a gray shirt and put it on. I rest my head back on the pillow. The pounding is now gone, thanks to the meds. I hear the door open and Ciera walks back in holding two Styrofoam containers in one hand and two bottles of orange juice in the other.

She lowers the containers down in front of me. "The top one is yours."

I grab it from her, and she starts to turn away, and her t-shirt rides up and I notice utensils sticking out from the top of her leggings.

"Hey, wait," I command.

She stops, turning around as I get up from the cot. Slowly, I make my way over to her; her eyes grow wide when I get closer. Ever since I opened my eyes, she's been there, and I find myself wanting to get closer to her. She doesn't move when I tower over her. Pushing my luck, I reach down and lift her shirt. Our gazes lock when my knuckles brush her warm skin and I hear her sharp intake of breath as I wrap my fingers around the utensil packet.

She sucks that bottom lip between her teeth. Fuck. It looks so much hotter when she does it.

Getting control of myself, I take a step back and hold it up. "You forgot this."

She lets out the breath that she had been holding. "Oh, sorry."

I see her flush a bright red, and she quickly turns and heads back to the desk. I sit back down on the bed and place the container in my lap, opening it up.

"Wow, this looks amazing," I remark as I undo the plastic wrap around the utensils.

"I know. I love the food the ladies make. Wait until you try the bacon!" Ciera says before taking a bite of eggs.

I look back down at my waffles, scrambled eggs, sausage, and bacon. I pick up a slice of bacon and take a bite.

"Oh, wow. That is fucking good!" I exclaim.

"I told you. I swear they put crack in it." Ciera laughs, and for some reason, my cock stirs.

I've heard plenty of women laugh before, but none of them have ever made my dick happy. Ignoring it, I take a few more bites of food.

"So, Ciera, how old are you?" I ask, wanting to fill the silence, but also wanting to talk to her.

"I'm twenty. You?" she asks, taking another bite.

I like the fact that this girl isn't shy around food. Most girls will order a salad when they really want a burger, and when they eat a salad, after a few bites, they say they're full. I mean, come on. I've eaten rabbit food before, and it takes the whole thing to make me feel full.

"Twenty-one," I answer. "What do you do? Are you still in school?"

Her face lights up. "No, I graduated early. I teach the kids here at the Compound."

I lift a brow. "Compound?"

She flushes. "It's a safe haven for witches."

It's all she says, but I believe her.

"You mentioned Abby earlier. Is she a—"

Ciera cuts me off. "Yes, Abby is a witch. But you didn't hear that from me."

"Your secret is safe with me." I smile.

She blushes again. I like seeing her blush. It's cute.

"So, you like teaching?" I prod, wanting to keep her talking.

I never usually care for the small talk, but this girl...she intrigues me. I actually want her to keep talking.

"I love it. I teach ages three to eight. I love watching their excitement when they learn something new, or when they finally do something that they've been struggling with. I love their curiosity, and I love all their personalities. Tucker, my youngest, stuck a Lego in his nose yesterday, but he's also the sweetest little boy. He shares everything. Maggie, one of my oldest girls, she's the princess, but she has a rough life. Her parents work a lot to maintain their store down in the Quarter." She stops and looks over at me. "I'm sorry. I'm rambling."

I laugh. "It's okay. It's nice that you care so much. I wish most teachers cared the way you do. I loved school, but some of the teachers just didn't give a shit. Many of them passed students just to move them along. Maybe if they actually cared, some people would have turned out differently."

She smiles. "I agree. I want my students to take pride in not only their work, but themselves. I also tell them it's not a race and everyone learns at their own pace."

Wow.

This girl is remarkable, and I only just met her.

"I like that." I smile and watch as she shoves another forkful of food into her mouth. "I've always been a quick study. Once I learned something, I was ready to move onto something else. I was going to go to school to study criminal law. But when I was looking at courses, I thought about taking a different path."

Ciera lifts a brow. "Oh yeah? What path were you thinking about taking?"

"Studying criminal behavior. Why criminals do what they do, so instead of putting them away, I would try to catch them instead. I don't know, it was just something I thought about. I didn't really tell anyone I was considering it because I wasn't sure if I wanted to do it. That's what college is about, right?"

Ciera laughs. "Changing your mind, then changing it again?"

"Ha, yeah, that about sums it up," I chuckle.

"So then what happened? Did you not go to school?" she asks.

There's a pain in my chest and suddenly I don't feel hungry anymore.

"I'm sorry. You don't have to answer. It's none of my business."

My eyes flick back up to hers.

"No, it's not that. My parents were killed, and everything changed," I admit, and glance back down at my food.

I start to think back on that night until I feel a hand on mine. I look back up and Ciera is now sitting in a chair right next to my bed.

"I'm so sorry for your loss. I can't imagine what you must have gone through." She gives me a small smile. "If you ever want to talk, I'm a pretty good listener."

"Thanks. I appreciate that," I reply. Unlike my sister, I don't mind talking about that night.

"What do you remember from last night?" Ciera asks.

"I remember running with my sister, meeting Hunter and Bennett in St. Louis Cemetery, and then I must have tripped and fallen," I lie, though I'm not sure why, since I know she's a witch. If she's a witch, then surely, she knows about vampires.

"I know." Ciera admits.

I lift a brow. "You know what?"

"About vampires. You don't have to lie," Ciera says.

"You totally just called me out on my shit," I joke, suddenly feeling relieved that I don't have to hide.

"I *am* a teacher. I know when I'm being lied to." Ciera points to my container. "Are you finished?"

"Yeah, I'm good, thanks." I hand it to her, and she throws it away.

Then, to my surprise, she walks back over to sit next to me, and we sit and talk a while longer. I'm not sure how long it's been when the door to the medical room opens and Ciera tells me Aria is here. I look over and see my sister walking in, her eyes glancing between Ciera and me.

"Well, I'd better go. Classes are going to start soon, and I need pick up the kids. I'm glad you're feeling better, Declan." Ciera smiles at me before waving goodbye to my sister.

I'm kicking myself for not getting her number before she left.

Aria waits until the door shuts, then she turns and narrows her eyes at me.

"She's a nice girl, Declan. Please do not hurt her," she scolds.

I roll my eyes. "I have no plans to. I genuinely like her. She's not like any of those other girls that I meet at bars. She's smart, funny, caring, passionate. Not to mention she's absolutely stunning."

I let out a sigh as I watch my sister's eyes soften. She knows me too well. She knows that I would never get into a relationship with a girl knowing that I wasn't going to stick around. But the issue is that I'm not sure if we are going to stick around.

"What happened out there last night, Declan?" Aria finally asks after a few moments.

I glance away for a moment before looking back up at her. "Honestly, I'm not sure. I saw Bennett getting thrown into you and Hunter. And before I knew it, the vamp had gotten the jump on me and then, lights out."

Aria reaches out and grabs my hand, giving it a squeeze.

"It's okay. You're lucky you got knocked out. I, however, was not so lucky. The son of a bitch bit me," she grumbles, pulling her hair to the side to expose the bite. It's healed, so all I see are the scars.

"I'm going to kill that motherfucker!" I shout, turning my face away from her.

I hate it when she gets hurt. I made a promise to my dad a long time ago that I'd protect her, and I hate breaking it.

"Well, that motherfucker is already dead. Hunter bit his head off," she tells me.

I whip my head back toward her. "Come again?"

"Right. You were passed out when he shifted. Hunter and Bennett are wolf shifters," Aria explains.

My eyes widen. Ciera told me they weren't witches, but I wasn't expecting them to be shifters.

"Oh, I'm not finished. Abby's here."

"Your best friend, Abby Thibodaux? Don't tell me she's a wolf shifter too?" I ask, playing dumb.

"She's not, but she is a witch," she says.

"Well, shit. Remind me never to get on her bad side," I joke.

Aria smacks my arm.

"What? I'm joking," I say, rubbing my arm even though it didn't hurt. Abby couldn't hurt a fly, let alone a human.

"I mean, that's not all. Hunter's father is the Alpha, and I may or may not have told him off last night." Aria cringes and looks anywhere but at me. I narrow my eyes at my short-tempered sister.

"What did you do?"

My tone makes Aria look me in the eyes.

"Well, I-I mean, he said that he was going to erase our memories, and I just kind of...well, you know, flipped out."

I let out a sigh and run a hand over my face, letting my head fall back onto the pillow. Aria and I jump at the loud sound of the door opening. An older woman comes in, setting a bag down on the desk and starts to go through it. My sister and I exchange amused looks when we hear her curse under her breath. She finally notices that I'm awake and comes over to me. She looks a lot like Ciera and then I remember her telling me that her grandmother, Kora, is the coven's healer. She runs a few tests before giving me a clean bill of health. Then she leaves and goes into her office, closing the door behind her.

"Alright, bro, get up. Mrs. Thibodaux said she'd fill us in on everything once you were awake and got the all-clear from Kora," Aria says, pulling the blankets off of me.

I glare at her before getting up. When we leave the medical room, we hear a whistle that draws our attention.

Bennett is waving at us to come over, and I look over at my sister and see her flush. I follow her eyes and notice that she and Hunter are having a moment. I don't say anything as we make our way over to the table. We sit and have breakfast with them, even though I already ate. Hunter and I strike up a conversation about the Mustang my dad and I were going to work on and his Impala while my sister eats, and when everyone is finished, we get up from the table and make our way outside. Apparently, Luna wants to talk to everyone, and it has to do with me and my sister.

"So, Dec, how are you feeling?" Bennett asks.

"I'm great, man. Any idea what Mrs. Thibodaux wants to talk about?" I ask, side-stepping around my sister and Hunter, who have stopped walking and are seemingly deep in conversation.

"Nope. All I know is we are meeting with the Alpha and some of the witches. They don't tell me anything," Bennett responds.

"Gotcha. So, witches and wolf shifters live here?" I ask.

"Yup. We protect the witches from vampires, and in turn, they keep the Compound safe. We're like a cool-ass team," he says.

I know enough about witches to know that there are four types: air, fire, water and earth.

"Ciera's an air witch," I mumble out loud.

"Yeah, Ciera and her grandmother, Kora, are air witches. You're about to meet Grace, who's a water witch. Kat is an earth witch, and my boy Zayne likes to play with fire. Of course, you guys already know Abby. She's also an air witch." He stops in his tracks and looks at me for a moment, then smirks at me.

"What?"

"Oh, nothing. Let me give you some advice about the smartest witch. Don't mess with Texas." And with that, Bennett turns and keeps walking.

"What the fuck is that supposed to mean?" I ask, walking after him.

He doesn't answer because we reach a white house with black shutters. We walk inside and down a hallway and into a large room with floor to ceiling windows. There's a guy about my age leaning up against the wall, and Bennett leaves to go stand next to him.

"Please have a seat." A man sitting behind a mahogany desk points to a sofa in the room.

I sit down, and then he introduces himself and informs me that he is the Alpha of the New Orleans wolf pack.

A few moments later, my sister walks in and takes a seat next to me. After a couple of minutes, more people arrive. My sister's leg starts to bounce, which indicates to me that's she's nervous. I place my hand on her knee to try and calm her down.

When Luna starts to talk, I realize that the feeling I had last night was right.

Coming to New Orleans is changing our lives.

FIVE
CIERA

"Okay, guys, it's lunchtime!" I shout.

All the kids squeal in delight. They rush to the sink to wash their hands, and then when they are finished, they go to their cubbies to grab their lunchboxes.

"What do you got?" Thomas asks Tucker, each of them peeking into the other's lunchbox.

"Um, a peanut butter and bananner sandwich, some grapes, and fruit punch. You?" Thomas replies as Tucker looks in his.

"I gots a whole bannaner, grape juice and peanut butter and jelly wifout the crust," Tucker answers.

Thomas scrunches his nose.

"Tucker, would you like my apple slices?" Callie offers.

"I would!" Thomas shouts, raising his hand.

Callie hands Thomas her apple slices and he gives her the grapes. They always trade food if they don't like something their parents pack them. I look at my students and realize that one of them is missing. Glancing around, I notice Maggie sitting in the corner, flipping through the pages of a princess book.

I walk over and sit down next to her, making sure that I'm facing the other kids too. "Why aren't you eating, Mags?"

She shrugs and her face falls. "I don't know."

Then she goes quiet for a moment.

"I have some snacks if you're hungry," I tell her.

I glance up to see all the kids turning and looking. A smile grows on my face when they all gather up their lunches and bring them over to us.

"Here, Maggie, you can have half of my sam-witch," Tucker offers, taking half out of his bag and handing it to her.

Maggie's face lights up as she takes it from him.

"You can have some grapes!" Callie says, taking out a napkin, carefully placing it on the floor, and setting a few grapes down on it.

Thomas gives her some apple slices.

I see Tucker struggling with his banana when his big blue eyes look up at me. "Um, Ms. Campbell, can you please help me?"

I chuckle. "Sure, Tuck."

I take the banana and peel the skin off, then hand it back to him. He breaks it in half, only one piece is bigger than the other. He glances from one piece to the next, ultimately setting the bigger half down on the napkin for Maggie.

"Thank you." Maggie smiles at her classmates and eats her food.

When she looks at me, I can see tears forming in her eyes. I wrap my arm around her and give her a hug.

"Did you know that dinosaurs are egg-stink?" Tucker says, swallowing a mouthful of food.

"Do you mean extinct?" I ask, and he looks up at me taking another bite of his sandwich.

He nods. "Yeah, egg-stink. A giant fireball came from space and smashed into the ground, killing all of the dinosaurs."

He raises his arm high into the air for effect. I have to hold in my laugh.

"That's not true!" Thomas says, taking a sip of his juice.

"Yes, it is! My daddy said it was," Tucker defends.

"Ms. Campbell, is it true?" Thomas looks up at me.

"Yes, it's true," I tell him.

"See. Ms. Campbell knows because she is the teacher. She knows every-ting." Tucker sets his sandwich down and takes a sip of his juice.

Callie and Maggie exchange a look, and I glance over at Callie's little sister, Peyton. She's just in her own little world eating her food.

Once the kids are finished eating, I tell them it's time for quiet time and to grab their mats. One by one, they lay them out on the floor and grab their blankets. Some kids don't take a nap, but they do let the others rest.

I sit down at the desk, open the book I was reading, and begin to read about demigods. It's all the things that I've already read, but I take my time with this chapter. Until I get to one paragraph that jumps out at me.

> *After Hercules, Zeus forbade any more demigods to be made, but that didn't stop the demigod gene from being passed down through the generations. A demigod's powers can only be activated by the god him or herself, or if dark magic is used. If descendants of Leto and Zeus have offspring, it should come as no surprise that a set of identical boy/girl twins will be born, effectively mimicking their counterparts, Artemis and Apollo.*

My eyes grow wide as everything snaps into place. Declan and Aria being identical, the power that I sense in him, the amulet. I jump at the sound of a soft knock on the doorframe and look up at Luna and my grandma standing there.

"Ciera, can you step outside for just a moment? There is something I need to discuss with both you and Kora. Abby will keep an eye on the children for a few minutes," Luna whispers just as Abby steps through the door.

I nod, getting up from the desk. Once I'm outside and the door is shut behind me, Luna tells me exactly what I had just figured out.

Declan and Aria are demigods.

KORA AND LUNA HAD ASKED ME IF I COULD SIT IN THE MEDICAL room for a little bit, while they ran out into town for some more supplies. Abby offered to walk the children home, so I told my kids I would see them tomorrow.

The room is quiet while I read more on the Greek gods, but the door bursts open, and Hunter is carrying Aria into the room. She's pretty banged up from a sparring match, so I get her all patched up, then grab my books and head into the office.

Given how protective Hunter is over Aria and the fact that they keep glancing at each other, it looks like they would like a little time alone. Hunter seems to really like Aria, from what I can tell. I've seen him date a few girls, but he's never been like this with any of them before.

I'm not sure how much time has passed, but I hear some loud chatter going on out in the medical room, so I get up and walk out.

"What the hell is going on out here?" I ask.

"I'm two seconds away from punching a ginger in the face," Aria says, narrowing her eyes at Bennett.

Can't say that I blame her. I've felt that way a few times myself. One time, I actually did hit him in the face, and I broke my hand while doing it. My eyes catch Declan's and he comes over to stand next to me.

Bennett tosses the pillow on the nearest bed and leans against the doorframe.

"Bring it on, Blondie." He smirks at her.

Aria quirks a brow and returns his smirk with one of her own. "Don't tempt me with a good time, Benny."

They start laughing as Hunter gets up from the chair and heads for the door. He nods at Declan and I as he passes by.

"Later!" Bennett waves his fingers off his forehead and leaves the room.

"See you later, Blondie," Hunter says, and shuts the door just as Aria chucks another pillow.

"My sister has a better arm than I do," Declan whispers.

I look over at him, lifting a curious brow.

"I played football in high school. I was a running back."

"Oh, okay," I reply, pretending to have an idea of what that means.

"How was your day?" Declan asks, changing the subject, his face still red from training.

"It was good." I look up at him.

He's looking at me intently, and his eyes flash a dark green when I suck my bottom lip between my teeth.

"So, you're a demigod," I say.

He blinks. "It appears so. How did you know?"

"Luna told me," I reply, jumping up on the desk, and I suddenly feel a little guilty for lying.

Declan comes to stand in front of me as I hear the door shut. I glance behind him and realize that Aria is gone, and I'm left alone with him. I start to get butterflies in my stomach as he inches closer. He steps up to me and leans in close, placing his hands on either side of my legs. My breath hitches in my lungs as he leans in closer. If this was Kai, I'd be pulling away, but with Declan…there's just something about him that draws me in. I look at his lips, and I guess he notices, because the corners tip up.

In one swift movement, he's sitting next to me on the desk and our thighs are touching. I let out a shaky breath. He grabs my hand; his fingers wrap around my thumb and bring it over to my phone…wait.

"Hey, what are you doing? That's my phone!" I all but shout, reaching for it.

He leans back, outstretching his arm so I can't reach it.

"I know." He smirks at me.

I realize that I'm leaning on him, so I quickly get off him and sit back up. I can feel my face heating up. He jumps down from the desk and his thumbs type away on my phone. When he's done, he looks up and hands me back my phone.

"What are you doing tonight?" he asks.

"Lesson plans," I answer. "What did you do to my phone?"

"I put my number in it and texted myself, so now I have your number." He smirks again, and I find myself smiling. "Anyway, I'm training with Zayne tonight on the fire element. The Alpha and Luna want us to learn how to use our magic and start training."

"That makes sense, since your powers have been bound. You've never learned how to access or control it." I hop down from the desk and place my finger on the outline of his amulet. "This is stopping you from using your magic."

I look up at him, and he's staring down at me.

"I figured it out," I whisper, revealing the truth.

"What?" he breathes.

"What you are. Luna only confirmed it." I go to pull my hand away, but he grabs it, keeping it in place. "I knew what I was the moment I could understand words. But you just found out. How are you so...okay with all of this?"

He sighs, taking a step back. "I never said I was okay. I've just learned to go with the flow. My dad taught me that there are some things that would be out of my control, and I would just have to learn to accept what I can't change." He scrubs a hand down his face. "I lost my parents and found out that vampires are real all within the same night. Nothing ever compares to that, and I don't think anything ever will. So, finding out that I'm a direct descendant of Apollo and my powers were awakened by this enchanted amulet seems like a walk in the park." He laughs, but there's no humor in it.

Without thinking, I wrap my arms around him. He's startled for a moment, but then returns my hug. I just want to take some of his pain away.

"I'm sure they would be very proud of the man you've become," I whisper, pulling away, but my hands still rest on his chest.

"Will you stop by tonight?" he asks placing his hands over mine.

I find myself nodding my head. I'm not sure why I agree to go. Some might call it curiosity, and maybe it is, but I think it's more than that. Declan is one part mystery and one part danger, and both parts are calling out to me.

Declan looks like he wants to say more, but instead, he gives my hand a tight squeeze before releasing it and walking out the door.

Six

Declan

I had to get out of that room before I kissed her.

This girl is making me re-evaluate where I stand with relationships.

She knows what I am, and she figured it out all on her own.

Ever since I woke up this morning, I've been thinking about a lot of things. Aria and I have been out on the road for so long that I've almost forgotten what it feels like to even have a home.

Ciera is like finally standing out in the sun, after months of being under cloudy skies.

But I'm no good for her. Everything about her screams everything amazing and good in this world. I've fucked more girls that I can count and didn't even let them spend the night. I've got a darkness in me, and I don't want to take the light away from *her*.

I get to Luna and Abby's cabin and make my way into the kitchen.

"Hello, Declan! I hope training went okay for you," Luna says when she sees me.

"Yeah, it did. I was able to get out some pent-up aggression. I don't like it when vampires get the upper hand," I say, remembering the night my parents died.

Other than that vamp who killed my parents, only one has ever gotten the upper hand, and that was just the other night.

"Fair enough. Listen, Zayne will be running late, so you'll train with Kat and Aria until he comes to get you," Luna tells me just as Aria comes down the steps, so she repeats herself to Aria.

"Oh, and I will need your amulets," Luna adds.

Out of the corner of my eye, I see Aria's hand immediately go to the moon-shaped amulet around her neck. She and I share a look of understanding for a moment. We know that the amulets are the last piece of Mom we have, and we also know that Luna won't let anything happen to them. I excuse myself and walk into the living room when Abby and Aria start talking with Luna. I see my suitcase and grab a change of clothes and pull my phone out from my bag. I smile when I see a text from an unknown number, I immediately save the number in my phone.

Me: You're still coming tonight, right?

I set the phone down on the bathroom counter and strip off my clothes. It feels nice not having to worry about using up all the hot water. And the best part? Having enough room to move my 6'2" frame in the shower.

I finish in record time, eager to see if Ciera's texted me back. I find myself oddly disappointed when I check my phone to see no new message from her. I quickly get dressed, and when I'm just about to walk down the steps, my phone vibrates in my back pocket.

Ciera: Of course. I'll be there. I might be a little late, but I'll be there.
Me: Can't wait.

I slip my phone back in my pocket and we make our way over to a clearing, where we hand over our necklaces to Luna. I know my amulet will be safe with her; Aria struggles for a moment, but with a reassuring glance from me, she finally hands hers over too.

Kat begins to tell us how to summon the earth element, and just when I think I have it down, Zayne shows up and we walk off, leaving my sister training with Kat.

"Is summoning fire the same as summoning the earth element?" I ask as Zayne and I approach a fire pit.

"Sort of," Zayne answers, turning around to face me. "A witch that can summon fire can also sense emotions in people because fire is the only element that comes from an emotion."

"I take it you mean anger?" I ask. It doesn't take a genius to figure that out.

Zayne nods. "You're good. Luna told me you were smart." He forms fire in his hand. "You know how it felt when you summoned the earth element?"

I recall the humming I felt in the stick and nod. "Yeah."

"All right, cool, it's kind of like that. Only you have to latch onto something that makes you angry," Zayne explains.

I close my eyes and think of the night that vampire killed my parents. It makes me angry that there wasn't anything that I could do to save them. I think of my mother and how she didn't tell us sooner about who and what we were and what was out there. Then I start to feel like my blood is magma, scorching my body, until the heat gathers in my hand.

"Dude, open your eyes!" Zayne shouts.

When I open my eyes and look down, I'm holding what appears to be a fireball.

"Think you can send it to the pit? You've gotta be quick, though. It'll burn you if you hold it too long."

"How do I do that?" I ask, intrigued.

"Think of it like a football," a feminine voice says, and I turn my head to see Ciera walking toward us. "Feel it leaving your hand and going to the wide receiver. Only the pit is the wide receiver."

"You've been doing your research," I say with a smirk.

She flushes. Damn, it's cute.

"Maybe a little." Ciera smiles and takes a step back. "Go on, player, show me what you've got."

I wink at her, then focus my attention to the pit. I can feel the flames growing hotter in my palm, so I picture it as a football. Then, I throw the fireball into the pit, igniting the wood.

"Fuck yeah, dude! You're a natural!" Zayne comes over and slaps my shoulder. "Let's keep going!"

Zayne and I start a healthy competition of throwing fireballs into the pit. He warns Ciera to stay clear, and she does...until she doesn't.

She moves, and it grabs my attention just as I let the ball of fire go. The flames leave my hand, aimed right in her direction, and it's too late.

She cries out as the fireball hits her arm. When I start to rush for her, the flames are pulled from her arm, and I turn to see Zayne moving the fire into the fire pit.

"Oh, shit. Ciera, babe, I'm so sorry. I don't know what happened," I say, gently touching her arm. It's red and starting to blister.

"It's o-okay," Ciera stutters, but tears start trailing down her pale cheeks.

"No, it's not okay," I whisper, swiping a tear away with my thumb.

This shouldn't have happened; I should never have lost my focus.

"We have to get her to Kora. She'll know what to do," Zayne says.

I scoop Ciera up in my arms and we make our way to the barn. Zayne opens all the doors for us, and when we get inside the medical room, it's empty.

"Where's Kora?" I ask, gently laying Ciera down on a bed.

"I'm right here, what in tarnation—" Kora comes out of the office and takes one look at Ciera, then her eyes narrow in on me. "What the hell happened to my granddaughter?"

"It was an accident, Grandma. Please don't be mad." Ciera's voice is shaky.

All I want to do is hold her right now. Do for her what she did for me earlier: take the pain away.

Kora looks at all of us, nods her head, and then turns on her heel, running back into her office.

I go over and sit in the chair next to Ciera; she lays her head down, turning her face toward me. Her cheeks are wet, but she's stopped crying, and I'm not sure whether that's a good thing or not.

"Ciera, I'm—" I start to say, but am cut off by the door bursting open.

My sister rushes into the room with Hunter and Bennett right behind her. It doesn't take me long to figure out that Zayne must have texted one of them.

"Out of the way!" Kora shouts, pushing her way through the two wolves and my sister. "What happened?"

I grab Ciera's hand as Kora gently picks her arm up, closely examining the burns.

"It's fine, Grandma. I'm okay," she insists.

The sound of her voice just makes me feel even guiltier. The last thing I want to do is hurt her.

My voice cracks. "No, it's not okay. I'm so sorry, Ciera. I didn't mean to hurt you."

Her face softens when she looks at me, "I know, but accidents happen. I knew what would happen if I stayed, and I stayed anyway. I'll be okay." She turns back to Kora. "Right, Grandma?"

Kora nods and leaves to go grab some supplies. I wish I could make this better for her.

I wish I could take away her pain.

Something inside me awakens and instinctively I reach over. When my hand touches her burns, it starts to glow.

I can feel myself doing the thing I so desperately wanted to do. I'm healing her. Taking the pain away.

"Oh, my gosh!" Ciera shouts, lifting her arm up and looking at it closely. Then her shocked gaze meets mine and she lowers her voice. "Declan, you healed me."

"Well, I'll be damned." Zayne whistles, leaning in to get a closer look. "That's a nifty little power."

Kora comes back over. She hasn't noticed yet that Ciera is better now. Ciera tries to tell her, but she is so focused that her attempts go unheard.

"Grandma! Look," Ciera exclaims louder, holding her arms up and showing Kora that both are fine. "Declan healed me. See? All better."

Kora drops whatever she was holding and gasps, her eyes going wide.

"What? How?" is all she manages to say, and she turns her attention to me.

I shrug. "Honestly, I have no clue. All I know is that I felt really bad, and I wanted to make it better for her."

Ciera reaches for my hand, giving it a squeeze before letting go, and I find myself missing her touch, which is a first for me. Kora stares in disbelief for a moment longer.

"I need a drink," she says as she gathers up all the materials and turns on her heel. She sets them in her bag and then walks out of the room without another word.

Bennett raises a brow at Ciera. "Kora drinks?"

"Occasionally. Usually only if something freaks her out. Since she's a witch, there's not much she hasn't seen. Well, until today, that is." Ciera giggles, and its music to my ears.

"Glad I could help." I smile at her.

"Alright, what happened?" Aria asks, looking between me and Zayne.

"Well, I was teaching him how start a fire. He was doing pretty well with it, so we decided to try something a bit more challenging." Zayne is the one who answers for me, and I turn just as he shoves his hands in his pockets. "We tried to throw fireballs."

I start to feel guilty again, but Ciera squeezes my hand and gives me a tiny smile. Bennett snorts, drawing my attention to them as Hunter squeezes his eyes shut and pinches the bridge of his nose.

Hunter glances behind me. "Zayne, you know you aren't allowed to do that anymore, right? Or have you forgotten about the dumpster incident?"

"Yes, and if I remember correctly, your drunken ass told me to 'light the bitch up,'" Zayne chuckles. "Look, that night aside, I had it under control. I'm good at what I do. You know this."

Hunter stares at him for few moments, but then sighs. "I know. Sorry, Z."

Zayne throws his hands in the air. "Don't worry about it. I get it. Anyway, we were practicing that when Ciera showed up. And, well, I'm guessing you can put two and two together."

"Hold on," Bennett interrupts suddenly, and we all turn to him. "Didn't Luna say they would each get a power or powers like Apollo and Artemis?" We all look at him and he rolls his eyes. "Don't tell me you all forgot."

I didn't forget, but my mind has been preoccupied with the pretty blue-eyed blonde sitting in front of me. Ever since I woke up in this medical room, she's been on my mind.

Why can't I get her off my mind?

Aria gasps, bringing a hand to her mouth. "Oh, my God. He's right."

"Yeah, duh. And it seems as though our Declan here has the power to heal, just like Apollo," Bennett explains smugly.

We all stare at him in disbelief.

He taps his forehead with his finger and smirks. "What? I'm smarter than I look. I'm beauty *and* brains."

"You know what, Benny? I don't care what anyone says. You're not that bad." Aria pats him on the shoulder and smiles. "But wait, what power would I get?"

I wish I'd had the sense to research Greek mythology. I don't really know much about it other than what I was told today.

"Well, Artemis was the goddess of childbirth," Ciera answers for him.

Oh, no. No way. Aria had better not start popping out random babies now.

"But she's also the goddess of the moon, the hunt, and archery.

But that's all I know," Ciera quickly adds when she notices the horrified look on my sister's face.

"Have you ever tried shooting a bow and arrow, Aria?" Hunter's voice is soft when he talks to my sister.

I notice that his eyes glow when he looks at her, but then he blinks and the glow is gone.

"Well?" he prods.

Aria shakes her head. "No, I haven't. I've always used my dagger. Or anything else that was handy."

My sister does have a knack for making a weapon out of anything, and by anything I mean....*anything*. Like this one time when we were in North Dakota and it was in the middle of winter. Aria and I tracked these vamps back to this house, and Aria's dagger was lost in the fight, so she used an icicle, of all things, to piece the heart. As long as you can pierce all the way through the heart, you can kill a vampire. And I'll be damned if my sister didn't plunge that icicle all the way through until it poked out if that vamp's back.

"I'll show you. I'll talk to my father and see what he thinks. It's worth a shot at least," he says.

She nods then turns back to me, pouting. "Why do you get the cool power?"

"Guess I'm the favorite." I wink, making her scowl at me.

Our mom and dad used to claim that one of us was the favorite whenever we agreed to grab them something, like my dad's keys or my mom's purse. Aria claims that she's really the favorite, but she's wrong.

"I'll help you with your new power, Declan. I'll do some research and we can work together to help you be able to conjure it on command," Ciera tells me.

I nod in agreement.

She turns to face Hunter. "Tell your father that I'll work with him."

Once a final plan is in order, we all go our separate ways, but I want to make sure Ciera gets home okay.

Ciera and I are walking so close to each other that our fingers brush a few times. After the millionth time, I lace my fingers with hers, and she doesn't pull away.

I want this girl, and I'm not talking about just fucking her. Don't get me wrong; fucking her would be great, but she makes me want more. I've never wanted *more* before.

I walk her all the way to her door, and I realize that I don't want to let her go.

"Thank you. For healing me," Ciera says, sucking that bottom lip in between her teeth and looking up at me.

If I kiss her now, I'm not going to be able to stop at just a kiss. I reach up and cup her cheek, pulling her bottom lip out from between her teeth.

"You have to stop doing that, because every time you do, I want to take that lip between *my* teeth," I whisper.

I hear her breath hitch as I lean in. I know she's expecting me to kiss her, and fuck, do I want to, but I kiss the corner of her mouth instead.

"Good night, Ciera," I say. My voice is husky even to my own ears.

I release her cheek, then slowly back away from her and down the steps.

SEVEN
CIERA

A chime from my phone pulls me from a deep sleep. After Declan walked me back last night, I took a quick shower and went to bed. I was exhausted from pulling an all-nighter and getting burned and completely healed all within the same day.

Declan: GOOD MORNING. *KISSING FACE EMOJI*

I can feel my lips turn up in a smile and my face flushes. I just don't know what it is about him that makes me feel...alive.

Me: MORNING. :-)
Declan: WHAT ARE YOU UP TO TODAY?
Me: THE KIDS HAVE THE DAY OFF TODAY, SO I'M CLEANING THE SCHOOLHOUSE. YOU?
Declan: NICE. I HAVE TRAINING THIS MORNING, BUT I'M EXCITED FOR TONIGHT.
Me: WHAT'S TONIGHT?
Declan: I GET TO SEE YOU. *GRINNING EMOJI*

It takes me a second to remember that I'm working with him on his healing power.

Declan: Don't tell me you forgot? :-(
Me: How could I forget you?
Declan: You see, I don't think you can. Not after last night. If I would have kissed you, would you have kissed me back?

Would I have kissed him back?

It doesn't take a rocket scientist to know that this guy has experience. He makes my body come alive in a way that no one else has.

The answer to his question is yes. I would have. But I'm torn. Part of me wants to say yes, but the other half, the less experienced half, chooses a different route.

Me: No.

You're a liar, liar, pants on fire, Ciera!

Declan: Liar.
Declan: I'll see you later, Ciera.

Smiling, I get up out of my bed and get ready. I throw on a pair of shorts and a tank and slip into my favorite yellow flip-flops. Grandma must still be in bed, because the cabin is quiet. Looks like she had one extra glass of scotch last night. She can't hold her liquor like she used to.

Grabbing my thermos from the fridge, I fill it with cold water, then make my way over to the schoolhouse. The kids only have school four days a week instead of five, so it's nice having a little break in the week. Once a month, I'll do a good cleaning, since kids carry all sorts of germs and, well, they can also get pretty messy. I turn the stereo on, and Dierks Bentley's "Sideways" blasts through the speakers as I begin to clean.

I start to hear music coming from outside, so I turn down my stereo and walk over to the window. It looks like Knox has the training class outside today and they're playing a game of football. They are split into two teams, shirts and no shirts. It doesn't take me long to spot platinum blonde hair.

He's Team No-Shirt.

I may or may not have googled football rules and regulations yesterday afternoon and a little before I fell asleep. I know the sport, but I didn't know anything about positions or how to play. It looks like Axton is the quarterback on Declan's team because he stands behind the center, who I think might be Kai, but I'm not sure since the defensive line is in the way. I'm pretty proud of myself for learning the positions so quickly. The ball is snapped, and Axton drops back, looking for someone open to pass the ball to.

"Declan is wide open, Ax!" I say out loud.

Not that it would do me any good; he can't hear me. He throws the ball to Bennett, who fumbles the ball as Jasper tackles him to the ground. Jasper helps Bennett up and both teams move down the field. They got a first down. The ball snaps again, and Axton fakes the ball to Bennett, but instead hands the ball to Declan, who is quickly making his way down the field. I see Blaine leap into the air and wrap his arms around Declan's shoulders, bringing them both tumbling to the ground.

"Blaine is such a dick," I mumble under my breath.

Another snap, and Axton throws the ball to Declan, but Blaine tackles him before he can catch the ball.

No one says anything! That's pass interference! Are you kidding me?

My temper flares, and I'm out of the schoolhouse and marching my ass over to Blaine.

"Hey Ci-Ci—" Kai starts, but I ignore him.

I stand my 5'4" frame in front of Blaine, barely coming up to chest level with his 6'1" build.

"Well, hey, little witch. Care to be my cheerleader?" Blaine smirks.

I grab his face with one hand.

"If you're going to play a game of football, then play it right or get the hell off the field!" I narrow my eyes as his widen.

I wait a beat, then release his face. Then I feel all eyes are on me.

"Oh, shit! Didn't anyone ever warn you not to mess with Texas? Damn, son!" I hear someone say, but I don't see who it is.

I'm too busy searching everyone's faces until my eyes meet pale green ones. They darken as Declan steps forward, but he stops when Kai walks up.

"Let me walk you back to the schoolhouse?" Kai offers as I continue to look at Declan.

"Um, yeah. Sure. Sorry, guys." I flush.

As I let Kai lead me back to the schoolhouse, I turn and see Declan staring at us, his expression unreadable.

"Since when do you know anything about football?" Kai asks as we reach the front porch.

"Since last night," I reply, shoving my hands in the back pockets of my shorts.

My eyes flick back to the field, and I watch as Declan scores a touchdown. I can feel my lips turn up in a smile. He looks like he's in his element as he runs over and high-fives Bennett and Axton.

"I see," Kai says, following my eyes to see that they are on Declan.

I look at him, and a pained look crosses his features. My heart sinks, and I'm pretty sure I just heard his break.

"Kai," I start to say, but he shakes his head.

"Nah, I get it." He steps closer but doesn't look at me. "Don't let him break your heart."

With that, he kisses the top of my head and runs off. Declan is looking at me intently, but someone grabs his attention, and he returns to playing the game.

"Ugh!" I toss my head back.

I turn and head back inside to continue cleaning. After a while, I realize that I could use some new supplies, so I grab my purse and my car keys and start to make my way over to where my Jeep is parked. I will myself not to turn around and look behind me, but my body doesn't listen, and I turn. I don't see Declan, or Bennett, for that matter. Trying not to think much into it, I continue along the path.

"Going somewhere?" The sound of Declan's voice makes me jump.

"You scared the crap out of me!" I huff, clutching onto my chest, my heart beating a mile a minute. "What are you doing here? You're supposed to be training."

He points down to his ankle. "I twisted it."

My eyes flick back up to his. "You're full of shit."

"What would your students think if they heard those colorful words coming out of that pretty mouth of yours?" He cocks a brow, and I feel my face heating up.

"I would never say them in front my kids." I counter.

He laughs as he walks over to the passenger side of my Jeep. "So, where are we going?"

"*We* aren't going anywhere. *I'm* going to the store to pick up a few things," I say, climbing into the driver's seat.

"Well, I'm going with you." Declan hops in, and I kick myself for not putting my doors back on.

I sigh and turn the ignition. "Meant to Be" by Bebe Rexha blasts through the stereo as I put my aviators on and put the car in drive.

"I should have known. You are definitely a country girl," Declan laughs.

I look over at him and smirk. "Hang on tight."

EIGHT

DECLAN

Faking an injury to hang out with Ciera seemed worth it at the time, but now that I'm in the car with her, I'm second-guessing that decision. I thought Aria's driving was terrifying, but clearly, I had never been in a car with Ciera. I grab onto the "oh shit" stick as she peels out onto the main road.

"Do you have lead in those flip-flops?" I ask.

She laughs. Her golden blonde hair shines in the sunlight as the wind whips it around.

"Sorry. I'm not used to having passengers," she explains.

I cock a brow, remembering her and that shifter, Kai. Seeing them interact earlier made me feel an emotion that I very rarely have.

"And that makes it okay to drive around like you're trying to win a NASCAR race?" I joke as she weaves in and out of traffic.

At least she uses her turn signal, a thing my sister refuses to acknowledge the existence of, and it drives me fucking insane.

"Hey, you're the one who jumped into my car," Ciera points out, looking over at me for a second, then back at the road.

"My life is in your hands, Ciera." I look over her, and she's grinning. "So, what's up with you and Kai?"

I don't do jealous. Never have and never will. But I'll be a son of a bitch if I didn't want to beat the shit out of Kai today.

Her face falls. "Kai and I are just friends. I mean, he wants more, but I—"

She pauses, as if trying to find the words to say. Now that I think about it, Kai did seem upset after he came back from the schoolhouse.

"You don't," I finish for her as we come to a stop light.

She looks over at me. "No."

A sense of relief washes over me. I refuse to go after girls who have something going on with anyone else.

"What do you want?" I wonder.

She's silent for about a minute.

"Passion," she finally says. "I want passion and I want to take a lifelong adventure with someone. You know, what everyone wants."

I chuckle. "Oh really? Is that what everyone wants?"

"I don't know, but it's what I want. What is it that you want, Declan?" she asks as we pull into the parking lot at Target.

I look at her for a long moment, then reach forward and take her sunglasses off. Her blue eyes search my face, but I don't answer her.

I smirk. "C'mon, let's go shopping."

I help Ciera pick out school supplies and cleaning supplies. It takes probably three times as long as it should, because we get distracted in the slipper aisle. That goofy girl has me laughing so hard when she puts on lion slippers and waddles down the aisle because they're still tagged together. Then she drags me down the toy aisle and wants to get this mystery box. She claims the kids love it, but I can see in her eyes that she secretly loves opening them too.

We set the bags down in the back and I hold out my hand. "Keys."

She narrows her eyes at me. "You aren't driving my car."

I step up to her, her back hitting the back of the Jeep as I close the distance between us. I reach behind her and slide my hand into the back pocket of her way-too-short shorts, pulling them out. I can hear her sharp intake of breath as I lean my head down, my lips brushing her ear.

"Get in the car, sunshine," I whisper, then back away. I hop into the driver's seat and Ciera gets in the passenger seat.

"You've been spending way too much time with Bennett," Ciera says while buckling her seatbelt.

I laugh. "What do you mean?"

"He loves giving people nicknames. I didn't think you were the type." She shrugs, turning toward me.

"The only other person in my life that I call something other than their name is my sister," I tell her. "You just brighten up my life."

We stare at each other for a moment, and then we both burst out laughing.

"Wow, that was extremely cheesy," Ciera says in between bouts of laughter.

"It was, wasn't it?" I look over at her and tuck a lock of hair behind her ear. "It's the truth, though."

She tucks that bottom lip in her teeth, and I use my thumb to take it out.

"What did I tell you about that lip?" I whisper, and I can see her face starting to turn pink.

"I like 'sunshine,'" she admits softly.

I smile. "Good. Because I wasn't going to stop calling you that."

Fuck, she's cute.

We continue the drive back to the Compound, and when I pull onto the dirt road, Ciera unbuckles her seatbelt.

"There's something I've always wanted to do but haven't had the chance to do it," she says.

I cock a brow. "Then do it."

To my surprise, she stands up, and the wind blows her hair back. With a carefree expression on her face, she lifts her hands into the air and tosses her head back.

She's breathtakingly beautiful, and it's not just her looks that make her that way. It's everything about her. The way she carries herself. The way she talks about her students. The way she cares so deeply for them.

The way she stood up for me earlier was fucking sexy, but more so was the fact that she read up on football. All the girls that came to my games didn't know shit about the rules and regulations, but Ciera learned them all in less than a day.

She makes me laugh, and I forget about all the bad shit in my life. She makes me feel like my old carefree self again.

I pull off to the side of the dirt road, park the Jeep, and unbuckle my seatbelt. I stand up next to her, and she looks up at me.

"What are you doing?" she asks, her voice barely above a whisper.

"There's something I've been wanting to do, but haven't had the chance to do it yet," I say, leaning in closer.

"What?" Her eyes are looking deep into mine, like she's looking into my soul.

"I want to kiss you." I reach up and cup her cheek. *Please say yes.*

Her eyes flick down to my lips. "Then do it."

I close the distance between us, brushing my lips against hers. I give her one more chance to back out before I kiss her harder. I grab her waist, bringing her closer to me as I swipe my tongue across her bottom lip, and I'm not surprised when she opens her mouth to me. She tastes like strawberries and mint, and I savor every moment of this kiss. Her hands wrap around my neck, and a soft moan escapes her lips.

Fuck.

I need to stop or else I'll be pitching a tent in the Jeep. Nylon shorts are no good at hiding boners.

I reluctantly pull away, because the gods only know what I'd do if I didn't.

"We should get back," I whisper as she opens her eyes.

The blue is dark and stormy-looking, and her lips are a little swollen. Damn, its fucking sexy.

"We should," she whispers back and drops back down in the seat.

I sit back down and pull back onto the dirt driveway. I grab her hand, lacing my fingers in hers as I drive us back to the lot. I park the Jeep and we get out to grab the bags, then we start to make our way back to the schoolhouse.

"Oh, no." Ciera stops walking and stares ahead.

Her eyebrows furrow with worry and she continues forward. I follow her gaze and see a little girl sitting on the steps of the schoolhouse. She lifts her head, and as soon as she sees Ciera, she bursts into tears and takes off running toward her. She wraps her little arms around Ciera's waist and sobs into her shirt.

"It's okay, Mags. I'm here." Ciera runs her hand through the little girl's brown curls. "Let's go inside."

Ciera picks her up and carries her inside, the bags forgotten on the ground. I pick them up and follow them inside the school.

"Do you want to talk about what happened, Maggie?" I hear Ciera ask as I set the bags down next to the desk.

I look around the room and notice a light is on in another room. I can hear a faucet running, so I assume it's the bathroom. Then I notice a piano by the window in the corner.

"M-mommy and D-daddy a-are f-fighting again," Maggie stutters.

I walk over and stand in the doorway. Ciera is kneeling down in front of Maggie, wiping her face with a damp cloth.

"It m-makes me s-sad when they f-fight," Maggie sniffles.

My chest tightens and I want to make this little girl feel better. I know I was lucky to have the parents that I did, so it breaks my heart to watch a child be so distraught over something like this.

"Aww, sweetie, I know. You know it's not your fault, right?" Ciera tells her.

Maggie drops her face.

"Your mommy and daddy love you very much," Ciera continues.

I step into the tiny bathroom and kneel down next to Ciera.

"Hi, Maggie. My name is Declan," I say.

Her brown eyes peek up at me.

"I have an idea that might make you feel better. Want to know what it is?"

Ciera looks over at me, her curiosity piqued, and I wink at her. Maggie nods her head and I stand, holding my hand out to her. She looks up at Ciera, unsure if she should, so Ciera nods her head for reassurance. Maggie then places her tiny hand in mine, and I lead her over to the piano. I slide onto the bench in front of the keys, and Maggie hops on the bench next to me.

"I'm going to play you a song, okay?" I tell her.

Maggie looks up at me and nods.

Then I start to play a song I haven't played in a long time. I had written this song for my mom and was going to surprise her on Mother's Day. But I haven't touched an instrument since my parents died. Aria and I left almost everything behind when we hit the road after their funeral.

I think my mother would be proud of me, of us, if she were here now.

I feel a weight on my shoulder and a tiny hand on my arm. I close my eyes, letting the notes take over me as I continue to play. When I open my eyes, they connect with deep blue ones. Ciera watches me with adoration and awe, and knowing what she does to me, she sucks in that bottom lip between her teeth again.

I got a taste of her earlier, and now I crave more.

My heart felt like it had a fog around it. My body was cold. And no matter how many women I fucked, they never made me feel anything.

Ciera's light breaks through the fog, and her touch warms the chill in my bones. I feel something with her, and part of me wants to tuck tail and run from the unknown, but the bigger part of me wants to *stay*.

"That was pretty," Maggie whispers when I finish the song. "What's it called?"

I look down at her and smile. "It's called 'Maggie's Lullaby.'"

Her face lights up and she gets the biggest grin on her face. "A song named after me? I love it!"

"Anything for the princess," I say, remembering my first conversation with Ciera.

Just then, there's a knock at the door and two people are standing in the doorway.

"I knew we would find her here," a lady who looks like Maggie says. "Maggie, sweetheart, are you ready to come back home?"

These must be her parents.

"We can make cookies!" her dad chimes in.

"O-tay!" Maggie shouts, and we both get up from the bench. She gives Ciera a hug. "Thank you, Ms. Campbell."

She starts to run off, then stops abruptly, turns on her heel, and runs straight into my arms. I pick her up and she wraps her arms around my neck.

"Thanks for the song, Declan."

I wink. "Anytime."

NINE

DECLAN

"I guess I'd better head back into the medical room before Bennett comes to find me." I step closer to Ciera, hoping I'll get a "see you later" kiss.

"Marco!" Bennett yells from just outside the door, and when he opens it, he's got this huge grin on his face. "You guys are supposed to yell Polo. That's the whole point of the game."

"Polo," I deadpan.

Bennett shoots me a look. "I know you guys are twins, but could you not? I get enough sass from Blondie. I don't think I can take it from Blondie Number Two." He pauses for a second, then shakes his head. "No, I don't like it. I'll have to come up with something better. Something that doesn't sound like I'm calling you dick."

Ciera giggles. "Blondie Number Two is a mouthful."

Then her eyes widen and Bennett snorts from the doorway. I grin, leaning down closer to her ear.

"Sunshine, I am more than a mouthful," I murmur, then I slowly pull back, lean in, and kiss her softly before taking a step back. "I'll text you."

I leave her standing in the schoolhouse and walk outside with Bennett.

"How's that ankle of yours?" Bennett asks as we walk along the path.

"It's a miracle. Kora really knows her stuff," I say sarcastically. He and I both know I faked it.

"Look, Ciera is a good girl. I don't know how long you and Blondie plan on staying—which, by the way, you're always welcome to stay here."

We stop walking and he puts a hand on my shoulder.

"But don't start something with Ciera unless you plan to stay and see it through. She's not that kind of girl."

He doesn't say anything more and I'm left wondering what the hell he means by that.

We make a pit stop to see my sister and Hunter. He's teaching her how to shoot a bow and arrow. Well, teaching her to tap into her powers.

Aria struggles with major change. She always has. It's gotten worse since our parents died, but from where I'm standing, it looks like Hunter is helping her through it. I see the tiny exchanges between them and I'm getting glimpses of my old sister back. She's not so on edge anymore, and she's smiling and laughing more. She seems...happy.

Bennett drops me off at Luna's front porch and leaves to go do whatever it is he does, and I walk into the cabin and into the kitchen.

"Hey, Abs," I say, opening the fridge and grabbing a bottle of water.

"Hey. How was training?" she asks, her silver eyes sparkling and a mischievous grin forming on her lips. She tries to hide it by taking a sip of whatever she's got in that mug, which I would bet money is hot chocolate.

"News travels fast around here, doesn't it?" I take another swig of water, and she laughs.

"Yeah, it does. I never knew you had such weak ankles, Declan." She laughs even harder.

"God, you are just like my sister," I sigh, scrubbing a hand down my face. "Look, if I've gotta have weak ankles to hang out with a girl, then so be it. It was worth it."

"Hey, no judgment here. Hopefully it's enough to get you both to stay. I really did miss you guys." Abby sets her mug down, but spins it around between her fingers.

I walk over to her and wrap my arms around her. "We missed you too. I'm glad Aria has you back in her life. It was hard on her to not only to leave our home behind, but to leave you too."

"Yeah. I wish she would talk to me, you know?" Abby says when I pull away.

"Give her time. She'll come around, especially now that she has Hunter. He seems to be helping her," I tell her.

She nods, then scrunches her nose. "You know I love you, but you stink."

I laugh and give her one last hug.

"You love me! I knew it!" I say as she squirms in my arms, trying to push me away.

I do remember her crush on me back in the day, and maybe I had a crush on her too at one point, but we both outgrew it and have moved on.

"Ugh, now I'm going to stink!" she shouts.

I kiss her cheek. "I'm going to shower now. You've hurt my feelings!"

I place a hand over my heart as I walk out of the kitchen and into the living room to grab some clothes.

"You'll live!" I hear Abby shout.

I've just gotten out of the shower and changed into shorts when the door slams open and a pale, wide-eyed Abby is standing in the doorway covered in blood.

"Abby, what happened? Where's Aria?" I ask, my heart rate kicking up.

She's breathing heavily and tears are flowing down her cheeks, but she doesn't say anything.

"Abby, where is Aria?" I repeat.

Please, don't let my sister be hurt.

"O-outside," is all Abby can get out before I rush out of the door and sprint down the stairs.

A sense of relief washes over me when I see that Aria is okay, but that's quickly gone when I see Sloane lying on the ground, bleeding out from her neck.

"What the hell happened?" I ask, kneeling down on the other side of Sloane across from my sister.

"I don't know! We don't have time to take her to Kora. You have to heal her!" Aria snaps at me.

I shake my head. "What? I'm not sure if I can!"

She looks up at me and our eyes lock.

"You can. Just try. Please!" she pleads.

I look down at Sloane, not knowing if I can do this. I have this power that, until last night, I didn't know I had. I'm not sure how to use it or control it.

"Son of a bitch!" Aria seethes, looking back at me. "Heal her!"

Then she gets up and takes off running toward the woods.

"What the fuck?! Aria! God damn it!" I yell.

I'm about to get up to go after her, but I see Hunter and Bennett running up.

"We'll go with her!" Hunter shouts as he and Bennett shift into their wolves and take off in the direction Aria went in.

"Kora and Ciera are on their way!" Abby says, kneeling down next to me. "Declan, please do something!"

"I'm working on it!" I snap.

I never lose my cool. I'm always one step ahead of the game, working out all sorts of scenarios and their outcomes. But this, I never saw coming. I hate not being in control and not having a plan.

I close my eyes, and I slowly start to feel the power, so I open my eyes and hover my hands over Sloane's neck. I can hear her breathing easier, but she's not completely healed, and now I'm starting to feel drained.

Exhausted, I fall back, breathing heavily.

"What happened?" Ciera comes running up, dropping the medical kit on the ground next to Sloane.

"We don't know. We just found her like that," Abby says as I watch Ciera start to work on Sloane.

"That's a vampire bite, Abby girl. Now, both of you, out of the way! Let us work!" Kora commands.

Abby helps me up and over to the porch steps. I feel her arm drape around my shoulders as I put my head in my hands.

"Ciera, where's Declan?" I vaguely hear my sister say.

I lift my head up.

"Is she going to be okay?" Aria asks.

"It's been touch and go for a few minutes, but I think we finally got her stabilized. I'll need help getting her to the medical room, though," Kora explains while still working on Sloane. She's cleaning up the wound, and it doesn't look as bad as it did earlier. "Declan healed her as best as he could. If he wasn't here, we would be having a different conversation." She pauses for a moment to place a bandage over Sloane's neck. "Alright, let's move her."

"I've got it," Abby says, getting up from next to me and going down the steps.

Sloane's body rises from the ground and begins to fly in the direction of the barn. There's a commotion and I see wolves emerging from the woods. I'm too wrapped up in my own mind to pay attention to any of the conversations. Just then, a body comes to kneel in front of me, and when my gaze lands on Aria, I can feel my eyes start to fill with unshed tears.

"Declan, she's going to be okay. Kora said that you managed to heal the worst of it," Aria whispers.

I nod slightly, then start to vigorously shake my head, getting up quickly. I accidentally knock my sister back, but Bennett catches her.

"What's the goddamned point of having a power if I can't fucking use it properly?" I growl. "What if I hadn't been able to do it, huh? What if—"

Overcome with anger, I punch the post by the stairs. I feel hands wrap around my arm and gently tug on me to turn. I do, but I refuse to look at *her*. I don't want her to see me like this. I hate it when people see me get angry. But when Ciera places her hands on my face, I have no choice. The second I look into her blue eyes, a sense of calm washes through me.

"But you did. You saved her. If you hadn't been here, if you hadn't tried to heal her, she would be dead. If it weren't for you, my grandma wouldn't have been able to save her," Ciera says sternly.

I stare at her for a moment, then I place my hands on her waist, pulling her close as she wraps her arms around my neck.

"We'll work on it," she whispers against my cheek. "I'm going to check in on her and then I'll come back, and we will practice. I promise."

Then she kisses me softly, in front of everyone.

I try not to show affection in public. It gives off the wrong impression, to other people, and to the girl. But I don't give a fuck if people think that Ciera's mine.

TEN

CIERA

I take a shower, scrubbing the blood from my fingers and my arms. I've seen blood before, and I've tended to wounds, but I've never seen one this bad before. I really wanted to stay with Declan, but Grandma needed me to help get Sloane settled.

Once everything was set, I came back home to shower and get ready for my first training session with Declan. I put on a simple black dress and use my air power to dry my hair. I find myself looking in the mirror and realize that I'm getting dressed for a date.

Would this be considered a date? No. I'm just a girl in a dress. I'm working with him on his new power.

I pick up my phone and text Declan. I've been worried about him ever since I left him to go help with Sloane.

Me: ARE YOU OKAY?
Declan: YEAH...

His answer seems clipped, so I turn my camera on, make a funny face, and send the picture to him, hoping that will make him feel better. My phone starts to vibrate, and his name pops up.

"Hello?" I answer, surprised that he's calling me.

"You're cute." His voice sounds hoarse, and he still seems a bit off.

"Um, thank you?" I chuckle softly.

He goes silent. I have to pull the phone away from my ear to make sure I didn't lose signal.

"Declan?" I say.

I can hear his ragged breathing on the other end of the line. "Yeah?"

"Everything is going to be okay. I promise," I reassure him, and I'm fighting the urge to run to him.

"Yeah."

I get up from my bed, slip my flip-flops on, and go downstairs. I can still hear him on the line, but it's not enough. I need to get to him. I open the front door and stop in my tracks.

"Hey, sunshine," he says, standing in front of me. He drops the phone from his ear and hits the end call button.

"Hey," I reply breathlessly.

In less than a second, he closes the distance between us and crashes his lips against mine. He lifts me up and walks us back inside, kicking the door shut with his foot. He groans as his tongue swirls with mine, and his hands drop low on my waist. He tastes like Tennessee whiskey, and I'm starting to get drunk off his kiss.

He pulls away, resting his forehead against mine. "I just needed to hear your voice, but as soon as I heard it, I needed to see you. When I saw you, I needed to touch you. When I touched you, I needed to kiss you. Now that I've kissed your lips, I want to know what kissing the rest of you feels like."

I feel my cheeks heating up, but not from embarrassment or shyness. No, my body has never reacted like this to a man before. I've dated guys, but the furthest I've ever gone was second base. I'm not saving myself for marriage or anything like that. I just…I don't know, I wasn't ready. It's my body, and the decision to give up my virginity is my own choice. I just never decided to give it up to anyone.

I stand on my toes and kiss him again.

"You ready to get started?" I whisper.

"Do we have to train? Can't we just make out, see where the night goes?" Declan answers, pulling back.

I laugh. "No." I reach for his hand, and he willingly takes it. "C'mon, let's go."

I lead him up to my room and shut the door behind us when we get inside. He spins slowly around my room, before turning to face me.

"I take it yellow is your favorite color?" he asks.

"What gave it away? The yellow tapestry hanging on the wall, the yellow accent pillows, or the yellow blankets?" I smile.

"I'll take 'all the above' for five hundred please, Alex," Declan jokes.

I lift a brow.

"Alex Trebek?"

I shake my head.

"From Jeopardy?"

"Oh, that guy!" I say cheerfully, even though the name doesn't ring any bells.

"You still have no idea, do you?" Declan's lips tip up as I shake my head again and laugh. "Fuck you're cute."

He steps up to me, and my heartrate kicks up as the playful look in his eyes is replaced with...hunger. I inhale sharply and clear my throat. Do I want Declan? Yes, but he should know that I'm a virgin. But that conversation can happen at another time. That's not why we're here.

I walk over to my desk, pull out a pin, and turn to face Declan. "Let's start out small and go from there."

He nods.

I go to sit down on my bed, and he follows. "Okay, I want you to close your eyes, and focus in on the power that's inside you. It's almost like feeling the hum of the earth or latching onto an emotion. Your healing power is there. You just have to remember what it feels like when you use it. It can be an emotion or a feeling." I pause for a few moments. "Got it?"

He nods and opens his eyes.

Then I take the pin and prick my finger, wincing at the slight sting. It starts to bleed, so I hold my finger out to him. He holds his hand over my finger, and it glows a faint yellowish white. My finger feels warm, and when he pulls his hand away, I squeeze my finger and a little blood comes out.

He sighs. "Well, that's disappointing."

"Hey, don't get discouraged. You can do this; I know you can." I smile at him.

Sometimes when my students are struggling, I give them a little push. Suddenly, I get an idea and jump up from the bed.

"Let's get out of here," I say.

"We aren't allowed out without a buddy," Declan says, grabbing my hand and trying to pull me back down onto the bed.

"We're only going out back. We'll be okay."

I spin and quickly grab my silver dagger from my dresser and rush down the steps, Declan not too far behind. When we get outside, the sun is starting to set. I turn to face him, keeping my hands behind my back.

"Do you trust me?" I ask.

Declan lifts a brow. "Where are you going with this?"

"I have an idea, but I need you to trust me," I say, biting my bottom lip. I start to have second thoughts, but I push them aside.

"Okay," he finally says, coming closer to me. "I trust you."

"Good."

I pull the dagger out, and suddenly regret this decision as I plunge it to the hilt into my stomach. I cry out in pain as the blade pierces my insides.

Oh, my God. This hurts.

Not one of my greatest ideas, but I know this will work.

"What the fuck? Ciera!" I hear Declan shout as he rushes forward and catches me as I fall to the ground. "What were you thinking!"

He rips the dagger out and takes his shirt off to place it over my wound.

"N-no. You need to h-heal me," I murmur.

I'm beginning to see stars, which is weird, because the sun is still out.

"I can't!" he says, his breathing erratic.

I grab his hand. "Y-yes, you c-can. I trust you."

I fight to take a breath, knowing that if he doesn't hurry, I'll start to bleed out.

A muscle ticks in his jaw, and he closes his eyes. When he opens them, determination crosses his features. He removes his shirt from my wound and places his hands over my stomach. It starts to grow warm, then the warmth spreads throughout my whole body, taking away all the pain. I no longer feel like I'm gasping for air. After a few moments, the pain is gone, and I feel fine.

Declan gets up from the ground and walks away.

I slowly sit up, thinking that I'll still feel some pain, but I feel nothing.

He did it.

I look over at him; his back muscles flex with every breath he takes. I get up and make my way over to him, and gently wrap my arms around him.

"You have a very special gift, Declan. I believe in you. Now you have to believe in yourself," I tell him.

He reaches up and grips my arms. "Don't ever do that again." He turns, grabbing my waist and resting his forehead against mine. "That scared the shit out of me."

"It worked. I feel fine," I whisper.

"Good, because I'm not sure what I would have done if it didn't." He kisses me gently.

"Ready to keep practicing?" I ask.

"Yeah, but no more surprises, okay?" He cups both of my cheeks and kisses me softly once more. His lips linger on mine for a moment before he pulls away.

"Okay," I breathe against his lips.

After my push, he's able to call upon the power to heal, and he heals me quicker each time I prick my finger or give myself a smaller cut. His healing touch is warming my skin, but it's also warming my heart.

"All right, guys, grab your things. It's time to go home!" I shout.

The kids run and get their things from their cubbies.

"Axton!!!" Thomas shouts as he spots him in the doorway.

"Hey, little man!" Axton holds up his hand, and Thomas runs over and high-fives him.

"Dude! Are you our buddy? Ms. Campbell says we need a wolf buddy to walk us home. Jasper walked with us this morning, and he's like my mommy in the mornings. I told him he should get coffee because that helps her be happy in the morning." Thomas shrugs.

Axton laughs. "That's what I always tell him, but he never listens. Maybe he'll listen to you." He kneels down. "But I will remind him to drink a cup before walking with you guys tomorrow morning. How's that sound?"

"Mm-hm," Thomas replies smiling up at him.

"Are you guys ready to go?" Axton stands taller, and all the kids stand up straight.

"Yes, sir!" they all shout.

"What was that?" Axton cups his ear. "I don't think I heard you."

"Yes, sir!" they shout even louder this time, and Tucker salutes.

Then, one by one, they form a single file line and Axton leads the way outside.

"Ms. Campbell," Joey says, tugging on my arm. I glance down at him and he's still looking straight ahead. "Why is Bennett running like that?"

I follow his line of sight and see Bennett sprinting over to us. In all my time here, I've only ever seen him run like this maybe a handful of times. It was usually when the kids suckered him into playing tag.

"Ciera!" Bennett yells and I cock a brow when he reaches us. He looks down at Joey, nodding his head at him. "S'up, kid?"

"You're weird," Joey says and walks over to stand next to Callie and Peyton.

Bennett scoffs. "Yeah, well, you're weirder."

"Bennett!" I slap his arm. "You can't say things like that to kids."

"He said it first!" Bennett points at him.

Now it's my turn to scoff.

"What do you want?" I ask, crossing my arms over my chest.

"It's Blondie. It's an emergency! Something is really wrong, and we need you," Bennett says.

I uncross my arms and look over at Axton. I'd hate to leave him alone with the kids.

"Go. I'll make sure they get home safely," Axton says.

I glance over at Maggie. Everyone knows Maggie's situation and we try not to make a big deal of it, for her sake. Axton glances down at Maggie, then back up to me, and nods.

"Go, Ciera."

"Thank you," I say, and I take off running toward the clearing with Bennett.

When we get there, Hunter is holding Aria in his arms.

"Everything okay? You sounded worried, and then I got worried. So, I panicked and all I could think to do was grab Ciera and rush over here," Bennett huffs out as we come to a halt right by Aria and Hunter.

"I hate running," I say, clutching my side.

"I thought you liked it, given that boy you dated who was on the track team in school. You went running with him every Saturday morning," Bennett teases.

He just had to bring up Chad, the asshole I dated a few years ago.

I narrow my eyes at him. "Please don't make me punch you in the face for bringing that fucker up."

Bennett chuckles, which only irritates me even more. So I follow through with the threat of hitting him, in the stomach instead of the face.

"For God's sake, Ciera," Bennett groans, hunching over in pain.

I take a step forward, kneeling down in front of Aria. "What's going on? All Bennett said was that it was Aria and it's an emergency."

"I started getting a bad headache yesterday afternoon. Sometimes I'll get this super sharp pain that lasts for a few minutes before it goes away. That's only happened twice now. But mostly it's just a dull ache." Aria lifts her head off Hunter's shoulder, but then lays it back down.

"Have you taken anything for it?" I ask, reaching up and feeling Aria's forehead.

She doesn't have a fever, but she does feel a little clammy. She asks for some ibuprofen from her backpack.

Hunter looks over at me. "What are you thinking?"

I chew on my bottom lip, trying not to think about what Declan told me about doing that.

"To be honest, I'm not sure. It could be she's just exhausted and needs a day or so to relax and rest." I stand, brushing my shorts off with my hands. "Or it could mean that her magic is just overwhelming her. Sometimes that will happen with the younger witches. If they don't release some of their power, it will have side effects, which vary from witch to witch. I can talk to my grandma about it. See what she thinks."

"Okay," Aria agrees reluctantly from Hunter's lap. "Just please don't tell Declan about what happened today. Not until we know for sure."

The woman in me doesn't want to keep anything from Declan, but the teacher and nurse in me is big on confidentiality. The latter takes over and I nod in agreement.

They start to have a conversation, but my mind is busy. I'm starting to wonder if her headaches may have anything to do with her being a demigod or her relation to Artemis.

Just then, the boys share a look and I know that someone used the link. At the same time, Aria gets a sharp pain in her head.

"Huh. Weird," I mutter under my breath.

"What?" Hunter snaps.

At any other time, I would have glared at him, but I can see that he really has feelings for this girl, and it hurts him to see her in so much pain.

"Did you guys use your telepathic link just now?" I ask.

Bennett and Hunter share a look, then they both nod.

"What does that have to do with Aria's headaches?" Bennett asks.

"I'm not sure. Maybe nothing, maybe everything." I shrug, taking a step closer.

Aria turns her head slightly to look up at me.

"You are so going to hate me for this, but humor me," I sigh. "Try using it again."

"Are you joking? If using that around Aria makes her head want to explode, then no, I won't put her in any more pain!" Hunter yells at me.

"But if it is the reason, then I can try to help her faster!" I yell back.

I know he wants to protect her, but I can't help if I don't know where to start.

Hunter inhales sharply. "Alright."

He turns to his best friend and they share a look. Almost instantly, Aria whimpers.

"Interesting. Okay, now I have somewhere to start. I'll check in with you guys later." I turn on my heel and take off running.

When I get back to my cabin, I flop down on my bed. I hate that I have to keep this from Declan, but I also don't want to worry him in case it's nothing. I grab my pillow, cover my face, and scream into it.

After a few moments, I sit up, and my eyes glance at my calendar. Tonight is the one night a month I go out to hit the town and blow off some steam. I know it's not safe, but I need to get out for a bit. Coming to a decision, I get up from my bed, grab my phone, and text the one person I know will come with me, who is also one of the few people who makes me feel safe.

Eleven

Declan

Training today was rough. I love a good workout, but damn. Knox really knows how to take that shit to the next level, and the class was smaller because some of the wolves got called to start patrolling. Everyone is on high alert since Sloane's attack, which is understandable.

"The next time Knox says, 'Just one more set,' I'm going to kick his ass," Jasper huffs out from next to me.

I laugh. "Yeah, tell me about it. I thought Coach Moore was tough, but clearly I was wrong."

"Coach Moore?" Jasper questions as he pulls his dreads back and ties a hair tie around them.

"My football coach. Smart man, taught me everything I needed to know and then some about the game, but he was a total dick," I reply, pulling out my phone and seeing that I have a text from Ciera.

"That would be why you were kicking ass before you got hurt." Jasper uses air quotes when he says, "got hurt".

"I plead the fifth." I stand, unlocking my phone to read the message.

Ciera: I'm canceling our training tonight. But meet me at my cabin at our normal time. xx

"Ahh, the reason for the injury has just texted you," Jasper laughs, clapping a hand down on my shoulder. "Don't mess with Texas, man."

And with that, he walks away. Why does everyone keep saying that?

Me: Getting into trouble tonight, are we?
Ciera: Maaaayyybeeeee.

I smile. This girl is something else. Every time I think I have her figured out, she does something like this and throws me off balance.

Me: I'm in. See you soon, sunshine. *kissing face emoji*

I slip my phone down in the pocket of my gym bag and walk with Jasper back to my cabin. It doesn't take me long to shower and get ready, and before I know it, I'm walking with Knox to Ciera's cabin.

I knock on the door, and when it opens, Ciera grabs a fistful of my shirt and pulls me inside, slamming the door shut behind us. Her eyes grow wide, and she spins, reopening the door.

"Sorry, Knox! Bye!" she yells, slamming the door again.

She turns back around, a huge smile on her face, and she runs and leaps into my arms, wrapping her legs around me. She crashes her lips onto mine, and when she pulls back, my eyes drop down to the hoop nose ring.

"I like it." I admit, looking into her deep blue eyes. "It's sexy. Also, if you want to greet me like this every day, I wouldn't mind."

She chuckles. "I don't wear it every day. Usually only when I go out. Kids like to pull."

When she shrugs her shoulders, her hips roll, and my dick starts to pay attention to the movement. I've never had a girl wrap her legs around my waist when her clothes were still on. She pecks my lips again and unwraps her legs, and I gently set her down.

"I'm almost ready. Give me ten minutes," she tells me.

I watch her walk away. She's wearing leggings and a t-shirt, and it's leaving so much to my imagination. I sit down on the couch and wait for her. When she comes back down ten minutes later, my fucking jaw hits the floor.

Her long blonde hair is down, and there's a small braid pulling one side of her hair away from her face, but the rest is flowing as she walks toward me. A black lacy bra peeks through top of her white tank top, drawing my eyes down to her tits. She's wearing several necklaces at different lengths. And damn, those shorts. I follow her toned legs down to ankle boots.

"Do we have to go out?" I ask as she grabs her purse and wraps it around her body.

She laughs. "Yes. It'll be fun, I promise."

"I can think of something else that's fun." I wink at her, grabbing her arm and pulling her to me.

I slip one hand in her back pocket, and the other cups her cheek. I bring my lips to hers, and I gently push her head back so I can deepen the kiss. I don't think I could ever get enough of kissing her, but I want more. I drop that hand that was on her cheek down to her waist, letting my fingers brush the skin on her side, and slowly bring it down to the hem of her shorts. The tips of my fingers just slip into her shorts, and she sighs into my mouth, pulling away.

What is this girl doing to me?

"We should go," Ciera says, grabbing my hand and lacing her fingers with mine.

"Where are we going?" I ask.

I'm curious as to why she's wearing this sexy little number, but I'm also feeling that pesky emotion of jealousy again. I don't want anyone else to see her like this. Only me.

I let her lead me out to the parking lot, and we run into Axton, who is leaning up against her Jeep.

"I had a feeling you'd be heading out into town tonight." Axton pushes himself off of her Jeep and walks over to us. "You know the rule. No one leaves the Compound without a shifter present."

I mean I get the rule, and I understand the rule, but I'm a

demigod, for fuck's sake. And I've been out on my own with no powers for the last three years. But what the fuck do I know? I guess what the Alpha says really goes.

Ciera sighs. "I know. I'm sorry. I take it you'll be our escort tonight?"

Axton looks between the both of us and nods. "Yeah, but don't worry. I won't ruin your date. I'll keep my distance." He turns and heads to a black SUV. "I'm driving."

Date? Is this a date? I can't even remember the last time I went on an actual date. It was probably back in high school, and we more than likely went to see a movie. Which I probably didn't watch because I was too busy making out with my "date."

Ciera and I exchange glances and follow him. I open the door to the backseat for her, jump in the front seat next to Axton, and pull my phone out from my pocket.

Me: THIS IS AWKWARD. I WANTED TO BE ALONE WITH YOU.
Ciera: SAME, BUT IT'S TO KEEP US SAFE.
Me: I CAN KEEP US SAFE. I HAVE MY DAGGER WITH ME.
Ciera: I HAVE ONE TOO.

That makes me smile. With all the other girls, I had to hide what I was. With Ciera, I don't have to. It's refreshing being able to be myself around her, and to be honest, around everyone else at the Compound too. After my parents were killed, I felt lost and like the world had abandoned me. Now I'm starting to feel whole again.

Me: GOOD. SO, HOW LONG TILL WE GET THERE?
Ciera: NOT LONG. USUALLY THIRTY MINUTES.

"I thought you two were supposed to be training?" Axton asks, pulling us out of our little world.

"Everyone needs a break every once in a while. Why do you

think I give the kids an extra day off?" Ciera chimes in from the backseat.

"Touché." Axton laughs. "All right, you two can go back to pretending I'm not here."

"Will do!" I say.

Ciera giggles from the backseat.

We start to play twenty questions, starting with simple questions.

I find out that she loves ice cream and French fries, and I tell her about the kind of music that I like. She laughs out loud when I tell her that I listen to rap in the car with my sister just to annoy her. I don't really have a favorite type of music because I appreciate all forms of music.

I tell her my middle name is Tristan and she tells me hers is Paige.

But then we start to dig deeper, asking the tough questions and really getting to know each other.

Me: WHAT'S ONE THING THAT NOT MANY PEOPLE KNOW ABOUT YOU?

I see the three bubbles pop up that let me know she's typing. Then it disappears, then reappears.

Me: YOU DON'T HAVE TO TELL ME IF YOU DON'T WANT TO.
Ciera: NO. I WANT TO TELL YOU, BUT I JUST DON'T KNOW HOW.
Me: JUST SAY IT. WHATEVER IT IS.
Ciera: OKAY.
Ciera: I'M A VIRGIN.

I'm taken aback. Well, that would explain her pulling away from me earlier.

But does she really think I care about something like that? I mean, yeah, I wouldn't hook up with some random virgin I met at a bar. But Ciera is anything but random to me. I'd happily wait for her.

Ciera: I'M SORRY. I SHOULD HAVE TOLD YOU EARLIER.
Ciera: WE CAN TELL AXTON TO TURN AROUND.
Ciera: THIS WAS A STUPID IDEA.

Just then, we pull into a parking lot of a night club, but everyone is dressed like they are going to a rodeo or something.

"We're here. I'll be around. Just text me when you guys are ready to leave," Axton says, putting the car in park.

Ciera inhales sharply, quickly gets out of the car, and immediately walks around the car and goes inside without so much as a glance in my direction.

"She told you, didn't she?" Axton asks.

I look over at him.

"Look, I know being a virgin is a big deal to guys, but don't be that douchebag who stops talking to her just because she is," he says.

"How did you know?" I ask, getting a little irritated.

"Kai. He got piss-ass drunk a few nights ago and let it slip. He has it bad for her, but she never felt the same. I can see it in her eyes. She really likes you. So don't be that douchebag."

"Her being a virgin doesn't bother me. The fact that she *thinks* it does is what bothers me," I say, getting out of the car and walking into the building.

My eyes search the place, and I finally spot her on the dance floor, moving her feet and swaying her hips to "Body Like a Back Road" by Sam Hunt, along with many others. They are doing some choreography to the song, and I realize she brought me to line dancing night. She tosses her head back in laughter as she dances with the people around her. She waves to people she knows, and they all walk up and hug her.

She's this sophisticated beauty with a carefree spirit, and I'm pretty sure I'm falling for her.

I set my eyes on her, and when I reach her, she looks up at me with trepidation. I lean down, closing the gap between us.

"It's not a stupid idea, sunshine. I'm glad I'm here with you," I whisper in her ear.

I pull back slightly and place a kiss on her lips, then we dance the night away.

"All right, cowgirls and boys! It's time to close out the night with a little Panic! at the Disco!" the deejay says.

Everyone hollers as "High Hopes" starts to blast through the speakers. The bass is thumping away, and bodies are packed close, everyone enjoying the sound of the music.

Ciera wraps her arms around my neck as we sing the song together. Then I start to get the familiar feeling that a vampire is near.

My body goes rigid.

I wish my sister was here. She would be able to tell exactly where it is. But she's not here, and I don't know where the vamp is. Just that one is near.

I pull Ciera off the dance floor and pull out my phone, texting Axton to come get us. He says he's right outside, so I keep Ciera close as we walk out of the building.

"What's going on?" Axton says as we reach his SUV.

I lower my voice. "A vampire is near. I don't know where, and I can't explain how I know, but you have to trust me."

Ciera gasps and tightens her grip on my hand.

"Get in," Axton commands.

I sit in the backseat with Ciera and she clings to me as we drive down the road. I still have the feeling when we pull into the driveway of the Compound.

Suddenly, Axton slams on the breaks, and Ciera and I fly forward.

"Shit. You guys have your silver daggers?" Axton asks, staring out in front of the car.

I follow his gaze.

"Oh, fuck," I murmur, my mind going to Ciera, and to my sister, who is out in the woods training with Zayne.

"I'll fend them off. You guys get back to the barn." Axton jumps out of the car and shifts into his wolf.

I climb into the driver's seat and am just about to put the car in drive when I hear a yelp. I don't have it in me to leave a man—well, in this case, wolf—behind. Axton has become a friend since our first sparring match. I can't let him do this alone. Not when I have the power to actually do something.

"Stay in the car," I command.

"What! No!" Ciera shouts.

I turn to look at her. "Ciera, *please.*"

She looks at me for a moment, then leans over the center console and kisses me.

"Be safe," she breathes.

"Get your dagger out and lock the door," I say, opening the door and slamming it shut behind me.

A locked car door won't keep a vampire out, but it will buy enough time for me to notice one is trying to break in.

I rush forward, and several vamps are ganging up on Axton. I reach into my pocket, pulling out my silver dagger, and throw it at one of the vamps. It hits him square in the chest, giving Axton enough time to attack. I pull my dagger out of the vamp's chest and am tackled from behind. I hit the ground hard, the dagger flying out of my hand, and I use the air element to bring it back to me. I elbow the vamp in the nose and use my body to toss him off, then plunge the dagger deep in his chest before using the earth element to summon a stick and stake him. A head rolls over to us and I look up to see Axton's wolf snarling.

Glass breaks.

I hear a scream, and my heart sinks.

A vampire is pulling Ciera out of the SUV, and she's trying to fight him off, but he quickly overpowers her. Before Axton or I can reach her, the vampire sinks its teeth in her neck.

For the first time in my life, I freeze. I didn't freeze when the vampire attacked my mother. I didn't freeze when I saw Aria being pinned by her throat in the cemetery. But now, seeing the look in Ciera's eyes as the vampire drinks her blood, I'm frozen in fear.

I can't lose her.

I'm knocked over by another vampire. My hands wrap around its neck, trying to hold it back from biting me. I feel the heat flow down my arms, and I start to burn its neck. Axton rips it off me and I jump to my feet. I look over to see Ciera starting to go limp.

"Ciera!" I shout and her eyes snap to mine.

She uses the last of her strength and stabs her silver dagger into the vampire's eye. He releases her at the same time as I use the air element to send them both flying into the air. I focus on Ciera, and instead of throwing her backward, I bring her to me. She soars into my arms, and I shift us, so she lands on top of me. I gently roll her over and remove the hair out of her wound.

"I'm going to make it better for you." My voice breaks as I hover my hand over her neck to heal her.

She gasps and coughs when I'm finished, then sits up. I cradle her in my arms.

"You guys good?" Axton asks after he shifts back into human form.

"Yeah, we're good," I say, my tone clipped.

Screams sound from the distance.

"We have to get back," I realize.

Axton shifts back into his wolf and makes sure we get into his SUV and we follow him back to the parking lot. I help Ciera out and get her into the safety of the barn.

"Are you guys okay?" Abby asks, running over to us.

"Yeah, we're fine," Ciera answers. Her voice sounds weak, but I know she's okay.

"I need to go help," I say, turning, and just when I go to leave the barn, the doors are locked. "Fuck!"

"The Alpha has these special locks installed that only lock when there's a threat. No one can get in or out until the threat is taken care of," Abby explains as dread filters through my entire body.

I need to get to my sister. One person I care about was injured tonight and I almost lost her. I'm not about to have the same, or worse, happen to the other person I care about.

Lately, it feels as though I'm failing to protect the people I care about. I failed as a brother, and now I failed at keeping Ciera safe. I could have saved her from being bitten, but I froze.

I don't like to fail, and I failed again tonight. And I refuse to let Ciera suffer for my mistakes.

Twelve

CIERA

The look on Declan's face after Abby tells him he's stuck in here breaks my heart. I look around, and I don't see his sister or Zayne anywhere.

I hear crying, so I turn and see Maggie sitting in the corner all by herself. I walk over to her and pull her into my lap.

"Shh. It's okay, Maggie. I'm here. You're safe," I coo, gently running my hand through her hair.

She clutches onto my arms, and I see Abby walk over to Declan. He takes one look at her, then pulls her into an embrace. A ping of jealousy washes through me.

They've known each other for years, right?

"Ms. Campbell, you're hurt!" Maggie shouts, and all eyes turn to us.

"No, Maggie, I'm fine. See?" I move my hair and touch my neck, then look down at my shirt.

"Hello, my lovely. I thought you might want this." Grace kneels down in front of me and hands me a t-shirt. "You go and get cleaned up; I'll watch her."

"No! P-please don't leave me! M-Ms. Campbell, please don't leave me." Maggie clutches onto my arm, and sobs into my shirt.

Declan's head turns at the sound of Maggie's panicked voice and he starts to walk over to us, with Abby right behind him.

"Mags, it's okay. I'll be right back. I promise." I place my hand on one of her cheeks and wipe the tears away.

Her eyes flick to the side and she spots Declan. She quickly gets up from my lap and runs straight into his arms, wrapping her tiny arms around his neck.

"Everything is going to be all right, Maggie," Declan tells her as he holds onto her tightly.

Our gazes lock for just a moment, then he glances down at my bloody shirt and before he looks away, I could swear he looks guilty. Like this is somehow his fault.

"You go get cleaned up. We will watch over her," Grace tells me, pulling me from my thoughts.

I trust that Declan, Grace and Abby will make sure she's okay.

I nod and stand. I know that Grandma will be in the medical room, and I don't want to face her right now, so instead I make my way to the training room. I push open the door, then head into the locker rooms. I grab some towels, walk over to the sink, and strip off my shirt. I turn the hot water on and let it run to heat up. I look at myself in the mirror; one side of my neck is bloody, but there's no evidence of a wound.

My eyes start to fill up with tears as I grab the paper towel and start to clean my neck, wanting to get the blood off. I've never been attacked by a vampire before. I've only seen the aftermath of the attacks, but to experience one firsthand is much different.

A sob escapes my throat as I scrub and scrub. When a firm hand covers mine and my eyes lock with Declan's in the mirror, I break down. He spins me and cradles my head to his chest. My body shakes as I cry into his shirt, and he holds me tighter.

A few minutes pass and I finally get control of myself. I pull back, and he finishes cleaning the rest of the blood off me in silence.

"My mom and dad wanted nothing to do with their gift. They never use their magic and they always yelled at me for using it. Grandma was the only person in my life that allowed me to be who I was. When we heard about this place, Grandma wanted to bring me here, to raise me in this life, because she knew the dangers of being a witch out in the real world," I say, filling in the quiet.

Declan doesn't say anything. He just continues to clean me up, and he heals all the tiny cuts on my body that I didn't even know I had.

"My grandma told them it wasn't fair that they were making the choice for me. She said I should be able to choose if I wanted to live a normal life or live in a world where I don't ignore the fact that evil exists."

Declan stands and helps me get into the clean shirt.

"Tonight was the scariest moment in my life," I admit quietly.

He cups my cheek and kisses me. I use my lips to tell him the things I'm not ready to say out loud.

I'm falling for you.

Please catch me.

But his kiss feels different. It's like he's saying goodbye, and that thought scares me because I finally found someone that I want to have a lifelong adventure with. I've only known him a short while, but it feels like I've known him forever.

Grandma tells me all the time, "Sweetheart, there will come a time when someone will walk into your life, and everything will change. When that person does, you hold onto them and never let go, because a love like that, it doesn't come cheap."

Somehow, I just know that Declan is that person.

He rests his forehead against mine. Then he pulls away, and I get a distinct feeling he's putting much more than physical distance between us. I jump down off the sink, and he grabs my hand, leading me out of the training room.

I look around and spot Maggie with Callie and Peyton. Their parents are keeping them together. Grace is nowhere to be seen.

"There you guys are. The vampires have all been killed, so we can go outside now," Abby tells us.

Declan starts walking faster toward the door.

"Where's Aria?" I hear Hunter ask as we finally get outside.

That's when I see where Grace went: she's standing behind Knox.

"What do you mean? I thought Aria was training with Zayne in the woods? Once the alarm sounded, this place was put on lockdown," Declan says, coming up and standing next to Knox.

"Knox, where are they?" Hunter asks again, more firmly this time. "I am not asking you again."

"There was a vampire in the woods where we were. We heard the attack and she told me to go." Knox sighs as Grace grabs his elbow.

Declan's body locks up as he stares off into the woods.

All of a sudden, there's a loud whooshing sound and I flinch as the heat smacks me in the face.

"Did my sister and Zayne come out of those woods?" Declan turns toward Knox.

The look on Knox's face tells us all we need to know.

"Hunter!" Bennett shouts, pointing toward the woods.

I look up to see Zayne carrying Aria out of the trees; her arm is hanging loosely to the side and her head is draped over his arm. Declan releases my hand and jumps off the porch, quickly starting to run in their direction. Hunter catches up, and then outruns all of us as we rush over to them.

"What happened?" Hunter snarls, looking up at Zayne.

"Aria created a distraction so I could get the flames under control long enough so this—" He waves at the flames behind him. "—wouldn't happen. But the vampire was about to bite her, so I hit him with fireballs. When he was down, I grabbed her, and we started to get the hell out of there. But then something happened with her head and she blacked out." He winces as he sucks in a hitched breath.

"Hunt, man, I'm sorry. I just needed to get us out of there." Zayne bends over, resting his hands on his knees. "He got away. I'm sorry."

Zayne looks up at Grace. "We need to get this fire under control."

She nods in agreement.

"Grace," Knox pleads from next to her.

"Knox Carter, you can wait here, or you can come with me, but

I'm going," Grace says firmly. She tugs her arm from his grasp, and we all rush into the woods to help put the fire out.

I've got my feet propped up on Grace's couch with a Greek mythology book in hand, trying to figure out what could possibly be happening to Aria and why she isn't waking up. We switched from Kat's cabin to Grace's, since their cabin is bigger. We haven't really figured out much, but we do think she's getting another power, so all of us are trying to figure out what it could be.

"Hello, Ciera!" Bennett picks my legs up and sits down, placing my feet in his lap.

Declan is with Luna and Abby. They set up a new cabin for him, so they are showing him around, while the rest of us continue to work. He looked like he needed to get out of here for a minute.

"Hi, Bennett," I say, turning the page.

"I'm bored," he groans, tossing his head back on the couch.

I set the book down and look at him.

"Did you finish your book already?" I ask, quirking a brow.

"Yes, and the only thing I learned was that Satyrs are half man and half goat, but that brought up a whole new set of questions." Bennett looks over at me and smirks.

"Do I want to know?"

"No, probably not." He laughs just as the front door opens and Declan walks in. "Where's Abby?"

Declan looks over at us. "She went to get Hunter. So we can fill him in on what we know so far."

"Okay, coolio. How'd you like your new cabin? I heard you got a new guitar!" Bennett says.

I look over at Declan. His hair is disheveled, and he has dark circles under his eyes.

"It's nice. Luna and Abby really outdid themselves." Declan

comes over and sits down on the coffee table, but he sits on the side farthest away from me.

"I didn't know you played the guitar." I only thought he played the piano.

"Yeah," Declan replies.

I wait for him to elaborate. When he doesn't, I pull my feet out of Bennett's lap and walk into the kitchen.

He's been extremely distant since last night. I know he's worried about his sister, but I'm beginning to suspect this might have something to do with me.

I don't think last night was the best time to tell him I'm a virgin. We were just getting to know each other, and maybe I dug a little too deep when he asked me to tell him something not many people know about me. At the same time, though, he needed to know. He seemed to be okay with it at the club, but maybe he's changed his mind.

Or maybe this is about me keeping Aria's headaches from him. I can understand where he'd be upset with me about that. I mean, she's his sister. His only family. I can tell he's protective over her. And I kept something huge about her from him. But if that's the case, why did he tell me it was okay in front of everyone?

I wish he would just tell me what I did.

Grace and Knox are cooking, so I sit down and start talking with Kat and Zayne. Moments later, Declan comes in and sits next to me. Grace gives me a sympathetic look as she turns to place some plates on the table. Even Zayne looks like he notices the tension between me and Declan. After a while, Abby returns with Hunter, and we fill him in on what we know.

Declan says he needs some air and leaves the room. I start to go after him, but Bennett tells me he's going to check on him.

As much as I want to go out there and see if he's okay, I sit back down. If he's mad at me, I'm sure I'm the last person he wants to see or talk to. And even though we're eventually going to have to talk about this, I know now isn't the time.

All the guys leave and follow Declan and Bennett outside, leaving us girls inside.

"What are we missing?" Kat asks, pouring herself another cup of coffee.

"We know that Artemis was the goddess of creatures," Abby starts to say.

"But that's not a power," Grace finishes.

Suddenly, it hits me, and it's like Zeus struck me with lightning.

"Oh, my God. That's it!" I all but shout, making the girls look at me. "When Bennett came to me yesterday and asked me to look at Aria about her headaches, I thought it was really odd that they would get worse when Hunter and Bennett would use the telepathic link."

Everyone stares at me like I have three heads.

"What if Aria's new power is being able to use the link like the shifters?" I elaborate and wait for everyone's tired brains to catch up.

"I think you may be right. But only time will tell. We should tell the others," Kat says.

I spring up from the table, hoping that good news might help Declan's mood.

"We think we may have figured it out," I announce, and proceed to tell them what the girls and I were just talking about.

"We won't know for sure until she wakes up, but it makes the most sense," Hunter says. "Nice work, Ciera."

I smile. "Thanks, but it was a collaborative effort."

"Well, thanks everyone. Now get some rest, please." Hunter turns and starts to head for the barn.

"I'm coming with you!" Declan shouts, and I watch as he runs after Hunter.

Everyone else disperses and I'm left standing alone on the porch.

I walk back to my cabin, and I can smell the rain in the air. I take a shower and lie down on my bed, pulling out my phone.

Me: HOW'S ARIA?
Declan: STILL THE SAME.

Me: I hope she wakes up soon.
Declan: Me too.
Me: Want some company tonight?

I want to be there for him. I can't imagine how this must be affecting him.

Declan: I'm hanging out with Bennett tonight.
Declan: I'll text you later.

I stare at my phone, feeling my eyes fill up.
Why is he letting me fall if he had no intention of catching me?

THIRTEEN
DECLAN

Standing at the kitchen counter in nothing but my jeans, I look at the alcohol selection, which is freshly replenished, since I gave Abby some cash to pick some stuff up the last time she went into town with her mom. I decide on the Tennessee whiskey and grab a glass from the cabinet, pouring the amber liquid in.

I lied to Ciera. I told her I was chilling with Bennett tonight.

Why? I don't fucking know.

This girl is everything. So why am I standing here, staring out the window at the rain, when I could be with her?

I've been doing things with her that I've never really done before: faking an injury to spend time with her, texting her whenever I get a chance.

She's the first thing I think about in the morning and the last thing before I fall asleep.

Even before our parents died, I wasn't the relationship type. The only other person I ever had anything with that I could even consider as being close to a relationship was this girl back in high school, Stefanie. But I chose sports and school and then she ended up moving to North Carolina. Last I heard, she was married now to a guy named Ethan.

A knock on the door pulls me from my thoughts. I down the rest of the whiskey and set the glass down on the counter and pad my way over to the front door. When I open it, denim-blue eyes are staring up at me.

Fuck.

Ciera is standing there, soaked, in a yellow sundress. Her usual golden blonde hair is now a dark brown from the rain. I step aside and let her in.

Apparently I can't avoid her even when I want to. And I *was* trying to avoid her.

She's everything good in this world, and I'm just not. Pain and death seem to follow me wherever I go. I couldn't protect my sister. I couldn't protect *her*. And I refuse to allow her goodness to be tainted by the darkness that surrounds me.

"How's Bennett?" she asks, whirling around and looking at me. She crosses her arms over her chest, pushing her tits up.

I look away as I walk past her and back into the kitchen. "Well, hello to you too."

That came out harsher than I intended. I can feel her eyes on me as I pour more whiskey into my glass and down its contents. I set the glass in the sink and grip the counter.

"I'm sorry," I sigh. "I didn't mean to snap. And I'm sorry that I lied to you."

"Why did you lie? Are you avoiding me?" she asks, her voice soft.

"No."

Yes. I lie. Again. Fuck.

I start to walk out of the kitchen, and Ciera follows me back into the living room.

"Did I do something wrong?" she asks, her voice sounding shaky.

I turn around to face her. "No."

That's the truth. She could never do anything wrong.

"Are you mad at me for keeping Aria's headaches from you?"

"No."

Again, the truth. Was I upset at first? Hell yeah, I was. But at the end of the day, everyone was trying to help her. I can't be mad at that.

"Is it someone else? I saw you with Abby earlier," she admits, wrapping her arms around her stomach.

My hands fall to my sides. "What? I've known Abby since I was a kid. We're just friends. Besides, I'm pretty sure she's been shacking up with Zayne."

"Oh," she whispers softly. "Then what is it?" She steps closer to me. "Is it because I told you I was a virgin?"

"You being a virgin has nothing to do with it."

"Then what? Please Declan, tell me what I did." Tears start falling down her cheeks.

"You didn't do anything, Ciera. That's just it. You're amazing. You make my world brighter just by existing in it. And I don't deserve that. You deserve so much better." Fuck. I run a hand through my hair. "I've been with a lot of women; I can't even remember their names. I couldn't even protect my own sister. I couldn't protect you! I don't deserve—"

Shit. This isn't coming out right.

Ciera's hands fall limp at her sides, the action cutting me off. "You don't have to protect me. I'm a big girl. I can take care of myself. But now I realize that falling for you was a mistake. I was just going to be another notch in your belt, another name you could forget."

"What did you just say?" I ask, not believing my own ears.

"Nothing. Just forget it. Forget me," she murmurs.

I clench my jaw and squeeze my eyes shut; I feel her walk past me.

What the fuck am I doing?

I turn and catch up to her just as she gets to the door. I place my palm flat on the door and push just as she starts to open it. She flinches as it slams shut, but she doesn't turn around. I can feel a shiver work its way down her spine from how close I'm standing.

I lean down to whisper in her ear. "I could never forget you, sunshine. You are *not* just some girl to me." I lower my hand to her shoulder and move her wet hair back from her neck. "You are so much more than that. What I feel for you, it scares the shit out of me. I haven't been avoiding you because you're a virgin or because there's someone else. There is no one else for me."

She turns her head and looks up at me through dark lashes. I glance down at her lips as she turns her body around.

"You got hurt because of *me*. The vampire that killed our parents has been looking for Aria and *me*. I should have never gotten out of that car. I've never been a boyfriend." I reach up and cup her cheek and bring my forehead to hers. "I always avoided relationships. In high school, I didn't want the distraction. But now it's because I don't want anyone to get hurt because of the life my sister and I live."

"Declan, if you hadn't been there, I would be dead," Ciera whispers. "My life will always be in danger, whether you're here or not. I feel safe when I'm with you, more so than with any shifter on this Compound."

My heart swells as I reach up and cup her cheek. "I love you, sunshine."

Her eyes grow wide at my revelation.

"I'm pretty sure I've been in love with you since the moment I met you in the medical room."

"What did you say?" she asks, her voice barely above a whisper.

"You heard me," I breathe.

She grips my wrist as I bring my lips down to hers. Kissing her is like a breath of fresh air. I swipe my tongue on her bottom lip, and she opens for me. My hands travel down to her waist, and I dip down and run my hand up her bare leg. I deepen the kiss and push her hard against the door. She brings her leg up and wraps it around my waist, and I let my hand travel up her dress to cup her ass. I feel her lace panties against my palm and groan into her mouth. She runs her hands through my hair as I pick her up, her back slamming into the front door again. My dick is straining hard in my jeans, and to my surprise, she reaches down and grips me.

"Fuck," I hiss as she squeezes.

I swear, if my pants hadn't been in the way, I would have come. That would be a record for me.

"Take me to bed," she whispers into my mouth.

I don't hesitate; I pull us away from the door and make my way up to my room. I kick my bedroom door closed behind me and lay her down on my new queen size mattress, not breaking our kiss.

I love this woman. And I want to make her mine in every way possible.

I slip my hand back under her dress and run a finger down the center of her panties.

"You're already so wet for me," I murmur, and she writhes under me.

I remove my hand and I swear I hear her whimper. I pull back and our eyes lock. Her lips are swollen, her eyes are hooded, and they darken as I go to pull away. She clasps my cheeks in her small hands, holding me in place. I adjust my weight, placing both hands on either side of her head. My arms are starting to shake, but it's not because I'm not strong enough. She's doing things to me, things that have me excited and nervous at the same time.

"I love you, Declan Matthews, and I want you. I've never been more sure of anything in my life. You deserve love. Please let me give it to you," she whispers.

My jaw clenches and I stare down at her in disbelief.

Our gazes lock, and she reassures me with a small smile before leaning up and pressing her lips against mine. I bring my knee up, placing it just between her legs, and push myself off her. I stare down at her, and she's looking at me with so much love in her eyes that it makes me forget why I ever started running from her in the first place.

I grab the hem of her dress and lift it up. She sits up so I can get it off over her head, then fumbles with the button of my jeans. I quickly grab her hands and hold them above her head.

"I'm making you mine in every possible way tonight," I whisper in her ear.

I kiss her neck, down to her collarbone, making my way down to her breasts. One hand keeps both her arms above her head, while the other comes down and releases one breast from her bra. I flick my tongue across the rosy peak, and she moans in response. I let go of her hands, and grab her other breast, releasing the other from the cup. I play with one nipple as I nip and suck on the other.

Ciera is writhing underneath me, pushing her chest further into my hands and mouth. I love how responsive she is.

I make my way down her stomach and kiss just above where the top of her underwear touches her stomach. She raises her hips slightly, begging me with her body. I glance up at her; our gazes lock as she watches me expectantly. I smile as I hook my fingers around the top of her panties and tug them down. I toss them to the side and push her legs open. I gently kiss the inside of her knee, making my way up to her sweet spot. When I finally reach the apex of her thighs, I hear her head hit the pillow.

She moans as I swipe my tongue down her center, then I insert a finger.

God, she's so ready for me.

Her hips come off the bed as I insert another finger, working her up to a climax. I place my palm flat on her pelvis to keep her still. I feel her walls clench around my fingers as she comes undone, and I catch her release with my mouth.

So fucking sweet.

I kiss my way back up her body, and she clasps the sides of my head, bringing me up to her lips and kissing me hard. I let her reach for the button of my jeans, giving her full control. I lean back so she can sit up and I watch as she unzips me and when my dick springs free, her eyes grow wide. She bites her lip and looks up at me. I could come just from that look alone.

That would be another first.

I reach down and grip the base of my cock, slowly stroking myself. I take her hand and place it under mine, guiding her along my shaft. Our gazes lock and I see a look of determination cross her delicate features. She nudges my hand away and then wraps her mouth around the tip of my cock.

Oh, fuck me.

I toss my head back as she takes me in her mouth, swirling her tongue around the tip as she goes down. I hit her teeth a few times, but I don't give a fuck. This is the best blow job I have ever gotten because it's from her. I run my hand through her damp hair as she bobs up and down. I refrain from thrusting my hips, letting her have all the control. When I feel my balls start to tighten, I gently yank her head away and bend over to kiss her.

I'm hungry for her now. I reach into my nightstand and grab a condom, quickly rolling it on before returning to kiss my girl.

She hooks a leg over my waist as I line my dick up to her entrance.

"I trust you," she murmurs.

I stare into her beautiful blue eyes. She's giving me all of her. And she's taken all of me. She will always have all of me.

I slowly enter her, inch by inch. Fuck, she's so tight. She winces and tenses up, so I stop moving.

"Relax, sunshine. I've got you," I whisper, before peppering soft kisses all over her face as I slide all the way in.

I don't move yet, knowing I need to let her get used to my size and being inside her. When she opens her eyes, she nods, letting me know it's okay to continue. I pull out slowly and repeat the process until I feel her hands on my lower back, pushing me in faster.

So, I give the lady what she wants. I quicken my thrusts, loving the way she feels. And it's all mine.

"Declan," she moans.

God, I love that sound. Especially when it's coming from her lips. I go faster now, not holding back, and she starts meeting me thrust for thrust. I catch her release with my kiss, then I bury my face in her neck, groaning as I come hard inside her.

Both of us are sweaty and breathless, but neither one of us lets go. I reluctantly pull back and look into her eyes.

She smiles up at me. "I love you."

I kiss her forehead, her cheek, her nose, then peck her lips. "I love you too, sunshine."

I pull out, kissing her as I do. I get up and head to the bathroom to dispose of the condom. When I come back to my room, I throw on a pair of gym shorts, grab my guitar, and pull up a chair. Ciera wraps my blanket around her, sitting up in the bed. I start to tune my guitar, getting used to the feel of having one in my hands again. Once it's tuned to my liking, I start to strum a song. It takes a few chords, but finally Ciera's face lights up.

"I know that song!" she says excitedly.

I continue to play "You Are My Sunshine."

"Is there an instrument you can't play?" she asks.

"Anything you have to blow into." I wink and she laughs. "To be honest, I've never actually tried to play anything other than guitar, piano, and drums."

"Apollo is the god of music and poetry. It makes sense that you're drawn to instruments," Ciera explains.

"Now I feel like my whole life has been a lie when you put it like that," I joke.

Ciera frowns. "I didn't mean it like that."

"I know you didn't, babe," I reassure her. "Do you remember the other day when you asked me what I wanted?"

She nods. "Yeah."

"Ask me again."

"Okay. Declan, what is it that you want?" She smirks.

"Well, thank you for asking. Let's see, I want passion." I smirk, then my face turns serious. "And a lifelong adventure with you."

I watch her eyes tear up, then she gets up from the bed, the sheet falling to the floor. I set my guitar down as she straddles me in the chair, her lips crashing down on mine. I grab her hips as she grinds into my growing erection, and for the second time in my life, I make love.

Fourteen
Ciera

"Ms. Campbell! Ms. Campbell!" Maggie says as she runs over to me.

She's finally found the plastic crown that I hid from her. She loves to play castle and make me the princess. Guess who's the queen?

"You need to put on the crown! It's time for a royal ball!" She forces the crown on my head, and I wince as the prongs stab into my skin.

I gently place my hands over hers. "Oh, is it? Here let me help you."

I adjust the crown so it sits on my head comfortably. Movement in the doorway catches my eye, and I look over to see Declan leaning against the frame, amusement all over his features.

It's been a few weeks since we admitted our feelings for each other, and we've been nearly inseparable ever since.

Maggie leans in close. "Oh, it's the prince!"

She was trying to whisper, but from the laughter in the doorway, I know that Declan heard her. I look around the room and notice the boys are playing with the Legos again, and I'm praying that Tucker is over the phase of putting them up his nose. Callie and Peyton come over and stand next to Maggie. The three of them are giggling uncontrollably.

Declan strolls into the room and up to me. "So, are you the queen and are these the princesses?"

Maggie snorts. "No. I'm the queen. Ms. Campbell is the princess. And Callie and Peyton are my royal best friends."

"Ah. I see. Well, then, Queen Maggie, if this is a ball, then where's the music? Surely, you have to dance at such a royal event?" Declan questions her.

He and Maggie have a growing friendship. He really cares about her, and when he's not able to make it to walk with us at the end of the day, he asks about her. She makes him play her lullaby from time to time, more so on the days her parents are stuck at work. He later told me that he originally had written the song for his mom, but then he saw how sad she was, and he wanted to make her feel special, to have something that was all hers.

"Good point, Prince Declan." She whirls around, and her eyes grow big as she sticks out her bottom lip in a great puppy dog look. "Ms. Campbell, the best teacher-slash-princess in the whole entire universe and beyond, can we please turn on the radio?"

She laces her fingers together by her chest and closes her eyes tightly. Callie and Peyton both give me the same looks. I have to admit, the girls are good.

"Well, we can't have a ball without music, can we?" I say, and I get squeals of delight from the girls.

I get up from my chair and turn on the stereo. Ed Sheeran's "Give Me Love" plays softly in the room. I turn around and see Maggie staring at Declan, who is staring at me.

I watch as Maggie slowly steps toward Declan. It's the first time I've ever really seen her so unsure of herself. It's so unlike that confident little witch. Then, I see her confidence peek through as she seems to give herself a little pep talk right before she tugs on the hem of Declan's shirt.

He glances down at her. "Yes, Queen Maggie?"

"W-will you please dance with me?" she asks shyly.

The other two girls giggle, which draws Declan's attention to them and then back to Maggie.

"It would be my honor." He bows to her, and her face lights up.

He holds out his hand to her and she places her tiny palm in his. Then he escorts her to the middle of the room. It makes me fall even more in love with him every time he interacts with my kids, especially Maggie.

Maggie giggles as Declan picks her up and she puts her feet on top of his, and he steps around in a circle with her. She's loving every minute, and I'd be lying if I said I wasn't starting to feel a tad jealous of a five-year-old girl.

"Queen Maggie," Declan says, pulling her attention from their feet up to his face.

"Yes, Prince Declan?"

"May I please have a dance with the princess?" he asks, and they stop dancing.

Maggie glances over at me, a smile forming on her tiny face. "Yes, that would be quite all right. Princess Ms. Campbell! The prince would like to dance!"

That gets the boys to look over. Apparently this, of all things, piques their interest. Go figure.

"I guess I don't want to disappoint the Prince or Queen, now, do I?" I ask, walking over to them.

"No, you wouldn't!" Maggie grabs my hand and places it in Declan's, then she pushes me into him.

I stumble into his hard chest, and he grabs my waist to steady me.

"Why hello, Princess Ms. Campbell." He smirks.

I shoot him a look, but I can't hold it, because I feel a smile forming on my lips.

"Shall we dance?" he asks.

I nod, and he leads me in a circle around the room. He twirls me, which earns us some soft "awwws." We don't break eye contact as we dance throughout the room, and I have to keep reminding myself that there are children present. The look he keeps giving me—it's like he's starving for me, and only me.

If the kids weren't here...well, let's just say I love it when he worships my body. I've never felt more alive than I do when he touches me and shows me just how much he loves me.

Right as the song ends, he dips me and the whole room erupts in applause. Declan is smiling down at me, then his eyes flick down to my lips, then quickly back up to my eyes. His pale green eyes search mine, and I'd let him kiss me if we didn't have an audience.

I break our eye contact for just a second to glance in the direction of the kids. Then I look back up at him. He starts to lean down, and I start to think he didn't get the message, but instead of his lips brushing mine, he places a soft kiss on my cheek. Then he stands us both upright.

There is a collective round of applause.

"Oh, gosh, they are perfect!" Callie looks on with a dreamy look on her face.

"Ms. Campbell and Declan sittin' in a tree! K-i-s....uh, Ms. Campbell how do you spell kissing?" Tucker asks.

I laugh and remove the crown from my head. "All right, everyone, show's over. Time to clean up."

"We're a hit," Declan says as he follows me back to my desk.

I pull out my lesson planner and shove it into my messenger bag.

"Are you coming over tonight?" he asks.

I freeze for a second, then continue packing up. "Yeah."

I've been a little nervous traveling outdoors since my attack. I know the grounds are safe again, but they were safe before and that didn't seem to stop the vampires.

"Sunshine, everything will be fine. I'll keep you safe. If you want, I can come over to you and then we can walk back to my cabin together."

I nod as he pulls my bottom lip out from my teeth.

"What do I keep telling you about that lip?" he mutters.

I can feel my body starting to warm up, and all thoughts of being bitten by a vampire again disappear.

"What if I'm doing it on purpose?" I ask, lowering my voice. "What if I like it when you bite my lip?"

"Ms. Campbell, there are students present." He leans in closer. "But if they weren't here, then I'd have you bent over that desk, and my cock would be so deep inside you, you'd be seeing stars in the daylight."

Oh, boy.

My face turns a bright red and I clench my legs together. I glance over at the kids, who are in their own little worlds, totally oblivious to me and Declan.

"You'd like that, wouldn't you?" he whispers next to my ear, sending delicious shivers down my spine.

I close my eyes as he places a soft kiss on my neck. He pulls away when we hear a loud noise, and I look over to see that Tucker's lunchbox has fallen on the floor.

"Look what you did, Thomas!" Tucker shouts, picking up his lunchbox.

"I didn't do it!" Thomas defends.

"Yes-huuuuh!"

"Nuh-uhhhhh"

"Okay, boys, that's enough!" I shout.

The boys stop, and I roll my eyes and look at Declan, who watches with amusement.

"I love it when you get all commanding. It's sexy." He winks.

I shake my head.

"I have a question for you. What other powers did Apollo have?" he asks.

"Um, well, apart from healing, his other active power was prophecy," I say, grabbing my messenger bag.

Axton is waiting for us at the door, and all the kids are hounding him with wolf questions.

"Why do you ask?" I close and lock up the schoolhouse, then start to follow Axton and the kids.

He grimaces. "Okay, don't be upset, but I've been seeing this woman in my dreams."

I stop walking and stare at him.

"No, it's nothing like that. I don't get a very good vibe from her. I've had dreams before, but none of them have been like this. I don't know. Maybe it's nothing." He shakes his head and starts to walk.

I grab his hand. "Hey, if your instincts are telling you that these aren't just dreams, then you should trust them. It's very possible that you picked up another power from Apollo. Typically, demigods only get one power, but it wasn't unheard-of for them to get two. Do you know who the woman is?"

"Not a clue. Maybe I can use my sister's paints and try to draw a sketch, or maybe ask her if she's home," Declan says, bringing our hands up to his lips and placing a kiss on the back of my mine. "I'll see you later, sunshine."

Then he leans in and places a soft kiss on my lips, remembering to keep it PG in front of the kids. We hear the boys yell "gross" and the girls squeal with "awws".

"Get a room!" Bennett shouts as he walks over to walk Declan back to his cabin.

I shoot him a look, and he hold up his hands.

"What? They don't understand what that means."

"My mom got a room with a friend once," Joey says.

I look down and lift a brow. I'm not sure why I always expect him to elaborate. He never does.

"You're a strange kid." Bennett laughs.

Joey looks up at him. "Takes one to know one."

And with that, Joey walks away.

"That kid scares me." Bennett watches as Joey walks over to Thomas and Tucker.

Declan laughs. "All children scare you, Benny."

"That's not true," he replies.

"Yes, it is," Declan and I say together.

"You two are adorbs." Bennett smiles, then pulls both of us into a group hug. "Ready to go, Declan?"

Declan nods. "Bye, babe."

He kisses me quickly before running off with Bennett.

If Declan does have a new gift, then I fear that the woman he's seeing is about to bring hell on earth.

FIFTEEN

DECLAN

When I walk into the cabin, I realize that it looks and smells clean. Aria must be doing her "performance cleaning," as she likes to call it. I can hear her singing in her room, so I walk upstairs and lean against the door frame. She's got a hairbrush and is standing on her bed. She turns and is only shocked for a half a second before she points at me and continues Survivor's "Eye of the Tiger."

I laugh and shake my head. I'm glad she's back to her old self again.

I go into my room and change my shirt and then sneak into my sister's new studio room. She's going to find it odd that I'm in here, because I never come in here and I never went into the room she had back home.

I grab some paint colors, not sure what the hell I'm doing or how to even mix paints. Music and instruments are my forte. Painting and art? Not so much. I grab a canvas, place it on the easel, and begin to paint.

"What are you doing?" Aria asks from the doorway.

"I've been dreaming about this girl for weeks now." I bite my bottom lip in concentration.

The action makes me think of my girl, and how I love it when she bites her lip. But I push those thoughts aside and focus back on the painting.

"Um, does Ciera know about this?"

I look up and shoot my sister a dirty look over the easel. "No, it's not like that. This girl...I get bad vibes from her. I'm just trying to get this image out of my head. Not that I think painting it will help."

I shrug. I'm not an artist, so I'm not sure why I thought this was a good idea. Aria comes over and stands next to me.

"Is this supposed to be a girl or a bear with a human face?" she laughs.

I scoff. "Aria, I'm serious."

I turn to her, and when she sees the serious look on my face, her face falls.

"Okay. Why didn't you just come to me? I can help you," she offers.

I don't know why I didn't think of asking her when I got home. It's not like she wouldn't have helped me.

Aria removes the canvas and places a new one on the easel. "Give me the brush. Describe her to me."

I hand her the brush and start describing the woman.

"So, are you glad we decided to stay?" I ask her while she paints the long dark hair on the mystery woman.

"Yeah. I think it's nice that we have people in our lives that know the dangers of the world and want to protect it just as much as we do," she answers, swiping the brush along the canvas.

My sister is amazing. I love all of her paintings and drawings. One Christmas, she painted me a guitar with watercolors. She included the lyric, "We are all just prisoners here of our own device" from "Hotel California," our favorite song by the Eagles. Growing up, that's all we listened to with our dad. I hung it on the wall by my bed.

"I agree. I'm happy here, more so than I've been in long time," I tell her.

"I can tell. Ciera is a huge part of that, and I'm really glad you didn't hurt her!" Aria playfully nudges my shoulder.

"I almost did, truth be told," I admit.

Aria stops painting to look over at me.

"What happened?" she asks, concern lacing her tone.

I know if I were to tell her I don't want to talk about it, she would accept that and drop it. She never forces anyone to open up to her, but I always do for the most part. She's always been one of my best friends, and even though it frustrates me that she won't really talk to me about *that night*, I'm glad she's finally opening up to someone about it. Even if it's not her full feelings, it's a start.

"The night of the attack, Ciera got bitten, and I froze. I froze for the first time in my life, and she got hurt. Then you got hurt, and I couldn't get to you. I was stuck in that barn and there wasn't a damn thing I could do about it." I scrub a hand down my face and close my eyes.

"Hey," Aria says softly, placing a hand on my shoulder. "Look at me."

I lift my head up and look at her.

"It's okay. I-I know what's it like to freeze up. I did it..." She pauses and sucks in a breath. "That night, I froze, and you got us out of Mom and Dad's room."

My eyes widen at her revelation and I reach up and place my hand over hers on my shoulder. I don't say anything as my gaze connects with hers. It's the first thing she's ever told me about that night. I'll take it.

Aria inhales sharply and forces a smile. "I'm glad you got over it, though. I can tell you guys are happy together."

She removes her hand and turns her attention back to the painting.

"You and Hunter seem pretty happy together too." I smirk when she glances over at me.

Aria flushes. "Yeah. I really like him."

"Like, really, really?" I joke.

"Like, really, really, big brother," she laughs. "He brings out the best in me and makes me feel like a better version of my old self. I know that probably sounds lame—"

"No, it doesn't," I cut her off.

She looks over at me and smiles.

I feel like things are finally starting to look up for us. Then I glance at the painting and see the woman who's been haunting my dreams lately and a sense of dread overcomes me. An hour passes and Aria is finally finished with the painting. She shows me the canvas and I feel the blood drain from my face.

"Yeah, that's her. I don't know who she is, but I don't like her. Whoever she is, she's bad news." I take the painting and place it on the table, not wanting to look at it for another second. "Thanks for helping me with this, little sister."

I grab Aria and pull her into a hug.

"Anytime." She wraps her arms around me. "All you have to do is ask."

I kiss the top of her head. "I know. I'm going to shower, then head over to see my lady."

I know Ciera is scared to walk alone, even though a shifter will be with her. So lately, I go to see her, and then we walk back to my place together.

IT'S BEEN A WEEK, AND A GROUP OF US ALL DECIDED TO GO SEE A band called Chasing Ghosts together. It's this all-girl band from the UK that Grace is a huge fan of. I'm just glad to be getting out of the Compound for a little while.

I'm sitting in the backseat of Hunter's Impala and my girl is sitting next to me wearing a black skirt, a maroon long-sleeved crop top, and ankle boots. Do I want her to straddle me right now, while I push her panties to the side and slide into her? Fuck yeah, I do.

My phone vibrates in my pocket pulling me from my thoughts and I pull it out, seeing it's a text from Ciera.

Ciera: I WANT YOU TO PICK ME UP HOW YOU WOULD WITH THE OTHER GIRLS.

I look over at her, and she blushes.

Me: But I already got the girl.
Ciera: Think of it as role play.
Me: I've created a vixen.
Me: I fucking love it. Okay, go inside and start dancing. I'll come to you.

I reach over and place my hand on her leg. If the engine wasn't so loud, I would bet she sucks in a sharp breath as I inch my hand higher. Then I pull my hand away.

When I first met her, she was this innocent virgin who was too smart for her own good. Now, she's a naughty teacher who is still too smart for her own good. She knows how to turn me on. Though, to be fair, it doesn't take much.

Me: Maybe I'll make you come undone.
Ciera: ;-)
Me: If you don't stop, it's going to get really awkward for my sister and her boyfriend.

I look over at her and she's biting her lip. I glance up in the front seat and notice that my sister and Hunter are having a conversation, not really paying attention to us in the back seat. I unclick her seatbelt, grab her leg, and slide her over to me. Her hand lands on my cheek as I lean forward and bite her lip.

"Game on, sunshine," I whisper in her ear as I kiss the soft spot on her neck.

Then I make her slide back over to her seat and she buckles herself back in. Her heated gaze connects with mine, and I wink at her.

We pull into the parking lot, and Hunter drops us off at the front while he goes and parks the car. I grab Ciera and pull her close to me, leaning down to whisper in her ear.

"You have no clue what you started. Go. I'll find you," I murmur.

Then I kiss her neck, darting my tongue out on the sensitive spot behind her ear. She pushes away from me and grabs Abby, and they go inside. Bennett is walking with my sister, and I spot Zayne.

"'Sup man? You ready to have some fun?" I ask.

"Hell yeah. But I need a drink first," he says.

I nod.

We show the bouncer our IDs and walk inside the crowded club. We make our way over to the bar and order whatever is on tap. I glance around the dance floor and spot Ciera dancing with Abby.

"She's sexy tonight," Zayne says, finishing his beer.

"Who?" I ask.

"Abby."

"She's a great girl. Go get her, tiger." I slap his shoulder.

He laughs. "You don't have to tell me twice."

Then he leaves and makes his way through the crowd to Abby. I drink the last of my beer and set the empty glass down on the counter.

It's time to pick up my girl.

I do what I always do and lurk back in the shadows, watching her. And slowly I make my way through the crowd. I come up behind her and wrap my hands around her lower stomach. She freezes, so I lean down.

"Hey, sunshine." My voice is pitched low as I start dancing with her.

At the sound of my voice, I feel her body instantly relax into mine. Abby and Zayne are off in their own little world, and it's just me and Ciera. The dance floor is packed with people dancing and grinding, and some people are even making out.

I lower one hand down her leg and reach under her skirt. I skim my hand higher, higher, and...there's my sweet spot. I start to swirl my thumb along the sensitive bundle of nerves, and she leans her head back on my shoulder, exposing her neck. I slide her panties to the side and slip a finger in, then kiss her neck as I insert a second finger. I hear her soft moan and I turn my head slightly and kiss her, swirling my tongue with hers.

"Ride my hand," I tell her as I feel her hips start to move in tandem.

I can feel her walls tighten and I kiss her, catching her release with my mouth. I always love doing that, whether it's from her lips or with my mouth on my favorite part of her. I remove my fingers from her, and she spins around in my arms. She kisses me passionately and I return it eagerly, using my lips and tongue to tell her how much I love her.

After a few more songs, the band comes on to play. I'm having a good time when I feel a tap on my shoulder.

I turn to see Hunter, and the look on his face tells me something is really wrong. The feeling I got when I looked at Aria's painting of the mystery woman comes back full force, and I look around, not seeing my sister anywhere. If she's not with Hunter, she's always with Bennett. But now, both of them are standing in front of me with worried looks on their faces.

"Where's Aria?" I ask, my heart starting to race.

"I don't know," he snaps as he turns and starts to walk toward the front door.

I grab Ciera's hand and we follow him and Bennett outside.

"Have you tried the link?" I ask when we finally get outside. It turns out that Ciera was right about Aria being able to use the telepathic link with the shifters.

"Yeah, but she's not answering. She went to the bathroom and when Abby went to check on her, she wasn't there," Hunter explains just as Knox, Grace, Abby, and Zayne all come out of the club.

"Let's spread out. She couldn't have gotten far," I suggest.

We split up and search the perimeter. My heart is racing, and panic starts to set in when I don't find her anywhere. When I round the corner and see Hunter standing there holding her boots, I'm pretty sure my heart stops beating.

"Hunter, why do you have her boots?" I ask, not really wanting to accept the answer. "Where is my sister? Why do you have her boots?"

I walk up to Hunter and he shakes his head.

"Has she been taken?"

Hunter nods. "I think so."

"Oh, God," I whisper, placing my hands on my head.

I feel a hand tug on my arm, and I look down at Ciera.

She places her other hand over my heart. "We *will* bring her back."

I cling to those words. Because I can't even think about the alternative.

"We need to get back to the Compound. We need a plan," Hunter commands.

He looks over at me, and I see a broken man with a determined look in his eyes. Ciera's right; we will find her. We have to.

We rush to Hunter's Impala and pile in, Bennett taking the backseat with Ciera.

"I don't understand. Why can't I use the link? It's almost like she's blocking me." Hunter grips the steering wheel, and I'm pretty sure if he grips it any harder, it might actually break.

"Blondie would never block you, especially if something has happened to her," Bennett reassures his best friend. "There has to be a reason..."

He cuts himself off, too afraid to say what's on everyone's minds. But call it twin intuition. I know she's still alive.

Ciera leans up in between us and looks at me, her eyes going right to my neck. "Take it off! The amulets are meant to help keep you safe, but it also binds your demigod powers!"

Trusting her, I take the amulet off, and the second it's off, I get this intense feeling in my head. I gasp, shutting my eyes.

"Declan are you okay? What's happening?" Ciera yells, climbing over the seat and plopping down in the middle.

Hunter swerves a little bit but regains the traction.

"I don't know, but I'm getting these images of a warehouse," I explain, rubbing my forehead.

"Kind of like that woman?" Ciera asks.

I nod.

"What does that mean?" Hunter makes a sharp right, then speeds down the road.

"We think he might have another gift," Ciera tells him, and tries to explain about my dreams while I continue to get flashes of this warehouse.

Then I see my sister. She's hanging from the ceiling by her arms. Her feet are in a bucket and she's been stripped of most of her clothing. The woman that we painted together is circling her and stabbing her with a dagger.

"Oh, God. Aria," I breathe.

"What? What do you see?" Hunter shouts as we turn into the Compound.

"It's Aria, and dude, it's bad. We have to find her as soon as possible," I say, not wanting him to know what's happening to her.

He doesn't need to know that. He doesn't need those images in his head. Hell, I don't want them in *my* head.

Once we get inside the barn, I describe to everyone what the warehouse looks like and have Bennett run to my cabin and grab the painting of the woman. I show it to everyone and let them know that she's the one who has Aria.

"They're alone, and Aria...sh-she's in bad shape," I choke out.

I need to keep calm in order to save my sister, so I reach for Ciera's hand.

"I know where that is," Knox says, looking at my sad attempt at drawings.

I'm just glad someone is able to make sense of that mess.

"That's not far from where we were at, its right off the highway. By that theme park," he tells us.

"Bennett, Declan, let's go. Knox, follow us, but keep your distance. We think the woman is alone, but we don't know for sure," Hunter instructs, starting to exit the barn.

I turn to Ciera and kiss her. "I'll be back soon, sunshine. I love you."

"I love you. Be safe," she says.

And with that, I take off after the guys.

Hunter is speeding down the road, and I can't explain it, but I know where to go.

"Turn here!" I shout from the backseat.

I'm just praying to the gods that my sister is still alive and holding on to the hope that these images are of real time and not the past.

Hunter cuts a sharp right.

"There!" I point straight ahead.

When we pull up to the building, I can sense a vampire, but the feeling is gone just as quick as it came. Hunter, Bennett, and I get out of the car and race to the door. Hunter is the first one to reach it.

"It's locked!" he shouts as he repeatedly kicks at the door. "Fuck!"

"Here, let me try," I say, getting an idea and stepping forward.

I place a palm on the steel handle, and the metal starts to glow orange as it heats. I fight through the pain. I will stop at nothing to bring my sister home safely...and alive.

I can't lose her too.

I let out a harsh breath once the door is good and hot. "Now let's try. On three."

"One," Hunter says.

"Two." I get ready to kick.

"Three," we both say at the same time.

We kick the steel door in, and the force of it makes the door fly off the hinges.

"You guys go. I'll watch the front." Bennett shifts as Hunter and I rush inside the warehouse.

It's dark inside, and the only light is in the center of the room. It shines down on chains, and some wet liquid on the ground.

Please be okay, Aria. Please be okay!

"I can't fucking see a thing," I whisper, trying to force my eyes to focus and adjust to the darkness.

I hear a soft moan coming from right in front of us.

"Holy fuck," I gasp.

Hunter and I spot her at the same time, and my heart literally skips several beats. In fact, I'm pretty sure it might have actually stopped beating altogether.

We take off running toward her, then my heart decides to play catch-up and then some.

Hunter's eyes glow around her and it's enough for me to see all the damage that the fucking bitch did to my little sister. I glance down and see the amulet hanging from her neck.

"Aria, little sister, can you hear me?" My voice breaks as I rip her amulet off and cup her cheeks.

I'm vaguely aware of Hunter taking his shirt off and ripping it to shreds. Normally, I'm the calm one in situations like this. But this is my sister, the only family I have left.

"Here, take some of these and tie them around the deeper cuts," Hunter commands, handing me strips of his shirt.

Hunter pauses for a minute, then looks over at me. "We have to work faster."

I vaguely wonder if maybe the link was used, but I push the thought to the side as I continue to bandage her wounds as quickly as I can. But, even though we're working as fast as we can, it still doesn't seem fast enough.

Once we're finished, Hunter scoops her up in his arms and we rush out of the building. I quickly climb into the backseat and Hunter gently lays her down in my lap.

Relief washes over me when I see the bleeding starting to slow down as we make our way back down the road. Her breaths are coming out shallow and uneven, and her entire body is ghost-white.

"You'll be okay, little sister. You're safe now. We're going home," I whisper to her. Not that I think she can hear me, but I hope she does.

I wish I could use my power to heal her, but Luna explained that since she's a demigod and can heal herself, my powers are useless.

Once we get back to the Compound, my girl and Kora are there waiting for us. Hunter carries her in, and Ciera walks with me to the medical room.

"Set her back in a room, Hunter," Kora commands.

"Take care of my sister, sunshine. Please," I choke out, and I can feel my eyes starting to fill up with tears.

"I will." Ciera kisses me quickly, and then rushes off into the room just as Hunter comes out.

His face is pale and he looks guilt-ridden.

"She's going to need you when she wakes up," I say when he approaches me.

I know she's been talking about our past with him. He told me as much when she was knocked out before.

"Aria doesn't handle trauma very well. It's been three years and she still hasn't dealt with our parents' death," I sigh.

"I'll do whatever it takes to help her through this," Hunter tells me.

"Good." I reply.

But I already know he would do anything for her. I can tell by the look on his face that he loves her. Whether or not they've admitted that to each other is none of my business, but I hope that when she wakes up, she trusts him enough to re-open old wounds and deal with the news ones too. I'll help him in any way I can, but somehow I just know that it's going to take more than just me to get her through this.

A FEW HOURS PASS BY, AND CIERA FINALLY GOES BACK HOME with Kora.

There's nothing more they can do for Aria. Her wounds are healing nicely, but she lost a lot of blood. I told Hunter to go home and shower, and he reluctantly agreed only because he needed to go update his dad on everything that went down tonight. We still don't know why Aria was taken, and we're hoping she will tell us when she wakes up.

I'm sitting alone in the quiet common area, so the sound of doors opening and closing catches my attention. I see Aria peek out and start to walk quickly through the barn. I get up and start to follow her, not wanting her out of my sight.

"Where do you think you're going?" I ask.

Aria jumps and whirls around at the sound of my voice. The movement is too much, and she cries out in pain. I didn't mean to hurt her, so I gently touch her, but she flinches away.

"Hey, it's me!" I hold up my hands. "You're safe now."

I lower my hands and glance down at her bare legs, which are covered in bandages. But I saw what that woman did. I know what's underneath.

"God Aria, I'm so sorry..." I trail off as tears start to fill in my eyes.

She's the only woman to ever make me emotional, except for Ciera.

I take a step forward, only Aria takes a step back, holding her hand up. She doesn't say a word, but it's written all over her face. She doesn't want to be around me or anyone right now. I nod, understanding her silent plea.

I watch her walk slowly out of the barn, and it breaks my heart to see her like this. I thought it was bad when our parents died, but this... This is so much worse.

I don't even know how we are going to help her get past this. I can't even imagine what she must be going through. I shoot a quick text to Hunter, letting him know she's awake and just ran outside.

"I hope she's okay."

I jump at the sound of Kai's voice, but I don't turn around. I watch as my sister heads toward the clearing with the fire pit, and I see a red wolf running after her.

"She will be," I reply.

"You know, I didn't like you at first," Kai admits.

I turn my head to him.

"I've been in love with Ciera since we were kids. But she never felt the same way, and I know she felt bad for never reciprocating those feelings. Of course, it never stopped me from trying." He laughs, but there's no humor in it. Then he turns to face me. "Her heart chose you, and I can't be mad at that. All I ask is that you protect it, and cherish her like she deserves."

I nod. "I will."

He slaps my shoulder. "Okay. Let me walk you to her, then. You look like you need a hug."

He laughs and holds the door open for me. Yeah, I could use much more than a hug right now. We start walking, and when I get to the familiar cabin, I climb the steps and knock on the door. When the door swings open, I'm greeted by the light of my life. My forever.

"Hey, sunshine," I whisper.

She glances behind me at Kai. I turn to see him smile and nod. Then he shifts into his wolf and takes off running into the woods.

Ciera takes a fistful of my shirt and drags me inside, shutting the door behind us. I hold onto her tightly, needing her strength and her love. I want to be strong for my sister, but right now, I can't. It's part of the reason why I let her go. I couldn't bring myself to be strong for her when I found her broken, bloody, and bruised.

I know Hunter will be strong for Aria. He's what she needs right now.

"You're home," Ciera whispers.

I know she doesn't mean literally.

She is what *I* need right now.

I nod, burying my face in her neck and inhaling my favorite scent of strawberries and mint.

"I'm home," I sigh.

The End

Also by Author

The Awakened
Rising Moon
The Gift
Rising Sun

Coming Soon!

Starting Fall 2020: Heroes of River Falls
An Interconnected Romantic Suspense Series!
Guarded Souls: Aubrey and Dean- Enemies to lovers
Reclaimed Hearts: Cassie and Dylan- Friends-to-lovers
Ignited Flames: Sophia and Bodhi- A (sort of) workplace romance
Stolen Memories: Chloe and Rhett- Amnesia-second chance

Starting Winter 2020: The Titan Trials-Bennett's trilogy

Light of Gods (Book 1)

Sea of Fury (Book 2)

Fate of Souls (Book 3)

Acknowledgements

Hey, readers! I hope you enjoyed Declan and Ciera's story! I truly loved their version of events in The Awakened. Thank you for taking a chance on their story and continuing to love these characters (and the new ones) just as much as I do.

Ciera-I know I thanked you in the acknowledgements in *The Awakened*, but since you are the real-life muse to Declan's love, you get another shout-out. Thank you for being you, and inspiring certain moments in this story, from the tiger slippers to the mystery box, you brought a young carefree spirit in this series. I'm so proud of you for getting good grades and getting all the scholarships into college. I'm so proud of you, babe! Love you!

Stefanie-My #1 alpha reader, and my long-lost bestie. Thank you so much for loving Declan so much and being there through all of my meltdowns this story gave me. You pushed me to make this story the best it could be, and you never let me give up. You are such an inspiring human being and Declan is really glad that his first girlfriend is you.

Katey aka Larry-My #2 Alpha! Thank you for listening to my crazy ramblings of all the plots from this book and, well, *Rising Sun* and Bennett's series. This book, and this series, wouldn't have been as strong if I didn't have you to muse mythology with. Thank you for always being there for me, especially when my phone decides to call you something else. Larry, I heart you!

Deborah K- You are a gem! Your support means so much to me and more. I'm really glad that I have gotten to know you and can call you a friend. Thank you for reading the extremely rough version of *The Gift* and still loving it. Please don't ever stop being your lovely self.

The Chaddettes- Ladies, you are the pop to my tarts. You've always been there for me no matter what. No matter where we are in the world, we still have someone awake to be a listening ear or to help cheer us up. My author journey would not have been the same without you. Y'all are the best, and I'm glad I've made lifelong friends.

Carmen-YOU ROCK. Seriously, you make my words shine! I think this was the roughest draft you've ever gotten from me. I told you that I felt like something was missing and after hours and hours of staring at my computer screen, you helped me pinpoint what was missing. Not only have I found a great editor, I've also made a great new friend!

BJ- Thank you for being one of the last sets of eyes on this baby and one of my closest friends. Also, thank you for being there for me as my biggest support system for *The Avengers: Endgame*. You get me. "I love you 3000."

Claudia- You can't have Declan. I love you, but he belongs to Stefanie.

Lena Ashani-Thank you for being the best cover designer. You always understand what my vision is and nail it every time. Thank you for always bringing my characters to life!

Angel-Thank you for also using your owl eyes to make this baby shine! I appreciate all the hard work that you put into proofreading. You always go the extra mile and beyond!

Clara-Thank you for always making the inside shine! The images, the scene breaks, and everything in between help make the story unique. You NAIL it every time, and I couldn't be happier with everything that you do. You're the absolute best, and a gem of a human being. Thank you!

And last but not least- Between the Covers: Amanda's Book Club, aka my Facebook reader group. Without all of you, this story, and the rest of the series wouldn't be happening. Thank you for always bringing a smile to my face. You guys ROCK.

About the Author

Amanda Carol lives in Westminster, Maryland, but has plans to move to Texas. She is a dog mom of one sassy little Yorkie named Raven (yes, after the Baltimore Ravens). She loves to travel and spend time at the beach. She enjoys writing about different worlds and bringing to life new characters. When she's not writing, you can find her binge-watching shows on Netflix, reading, or taking unexpected family trips to Target. If you would like to follow her and get updates on future works, you can click on the links below.

Website: https://authoramanda27.wixsite.com/website
Between the Covers FB Reader Group: https://www.facebook.com/groups/ACBetweenTheCovers/
Author Facebook Page: https://www.facebook.com/amandacarol27/
Instagram: https://www.instagram.com/author.amandacarol27
Amazon: https://www.amazon.com/Amanda-Carol/e/B07VB5PNRX

Made in the USA
Middletown, DE
01 July 2022